PENGUIN BOOKS

K: THE ART OF LOVE

Hong Ying was born into a sailor's family in Chongqing on the Yangtze River in Southwest China. An author and poet, she began her career as a full-time writer in the early 1980s having studied creative writing at Lu Xun Creative Writing Academy and Fudan University.

She is best known in the English-speaking world for her novels: *K: The Art of Love* (which won the Prix de Rome in 2005), *The Concubine of Shanghai*, *Peacock Cries* and *Summer of Betrayal*. Her autobiography, *Daughter of the River*, has been translated into twenty-nine languages and many of her works have been turned into television series and films. Her latest memoir, *Good Children of the Flowers*, a sequel to *Daughter of the River*, won *Asia Weekly*'s Top Ten Books of the Year Award in 2009. She lives in Beijing with her husband and daughter.

D1146967

BY THE SAME AUTHOR

Summer of Betrayal
Daughter of the River
Peacock Cries
The Concubine of Shanghai

K: The Art of Love

HONG YING

Translated by Nicky Harman and Henry Zhao

PENGUIN BOOKS

PENGUIN BOOKS

Published by the Penguin Group
Penguin Books Ltd, 80 Strand, London WC2R ORL, England
Penguin Group (USA), Inc., 375 Hudson Street, New York, New York 10014, USA
Penguin Group (Canada), 90 Eglinton Avenue East, Suite 700, Toronto, Ontario, Canada M4P 2Y3
(a division of Pearson Penguin Canada Inc.)
Penguin Ireland, 25 St Stephen's Green, Dublin 2, Ireland (a division of Penguin Books Ltd)
Penguin Group (Australia), 250 Camberwell Road, Camberwell, Victoria 3124, Australia
(a division of Pearson Australia Group Pty Ltd)
Penguin Books India Pvt Ltd, 11 Community Centre, Panchsheel Park, New Delhi – 110 017, India
Penguin Group (NZ), 67 Apollo Drive, Rosedale, North Shore 0632, New Zealand
(a division of Pearson New Zealand Ltd)
Penguin Books (South Africa) (Pty) Ltd, 24 Sturdee Avenue, Rosebank, Johannesburg 2196, South Africa

Penguin Books Ltd, Registered Offices: 80 Strand, London WC2R ORL, England

www.penguin.com

First published as *K* in Taiwan 2001
First published in Great Britain and in the USA by Marion Boyars Publishers Ltd 2002
Published in Penguin Books 2011

1

Copyright © Haashan Chubansher, Taiwan
Translation copyright © from the Chinese by Nicky Harman and Henry Zhao, 2002

The moral right of the author and of the translators has been asserted

All rights reserved
Without limiting the rights under copyright
reserved above, no part of this publication may be
reproduced, stored in or introduced into a retrieval system,
or transmitted, in any form or by any means (electronic, mechanical,
photocopying, recording or otherwise), without the prior
written permission of both the copyright owner and
the above publisher of this book

Printed in Great Britain by Clays Ltd, St Ives plc

A CIP catalogue record for this book is available from the British Library

ISBN: 978-0-241-95069-2

www.greenpenguin.co.uk

Penguin Books is committed to a sustainable future
for our business, our readers and our planet.
The book in your hands is made from paper
certified by the Forest Stewardship Council.

FT
Pbk

Author's Foreword

As far as the creation of a novel goes, I believe there is only one basic criterion: a novel should be 'a good story well told'. This should be in the forefront of one's mind before and during the writing. After the book is written it is, of course, too late to do anything except re-read and review one's feelings about it.

Since *K* is based on a true story I will first explain how it came about. In China in the 1980s I was involved in both officially recognized and underground literary circles. I was reading voraciously and one of the first writers I came across was the chief protagonist of the book – that is, K herself. I very much admired her highly evocative, romantic writings – to me she was the boldest of the New Moon Society's women authors.

In the course of time, tantalizingly sketchy rumours about K's life also came to my ears. Although it was hard to be certain how true they were, they linked her to a certain young English poet by the name of Julian Bell, son of Vanessa Bell and nephew of Virginia Woolf. I came across people loosely connected with K, one of whom was a student of Julian's at Wuhan University. He it was who went with Julian to Sichuan to look for the Red Army. This man later became a well-known writer and translator and, in the 1980s, published lengthy memoirs, which included a few words about his old teacher, Julian Bell.

I saw pictures of K, which did indeed show her to be exceptionally beautiful, and I came across contemporary biographies which refer to her as the Beauty of Luojia Hill. I have also seen photographs of her wearing glasses, and these appear to transform her magically into a typical 'woman writer'.

This, of course, did not make a story, but it did make a deep impression on me.

In 1994, Bloomsbury brought out a thick volume of the collected letters of Vanessa Bell. These included many letters to her son Julian, in which K was frequently mentioned, and the extent of the loving intimacy between mother and son that these letters reveal was very moving. Her country home, Charleston, attracts a constant stream of Bloomsbury scholars from all over the world. Inside the house, on the walls decorated with Bell's paintings, it is the portraits of Julian that dominate. Walking from room to room on a visit to the house, I was intrigued to notice a number of Chinese works of art, which might well have been presents from Julian to his mother: two bronze antiques, for example, and a statue of the Bodhisattva Guan Yin.

I had decided to dig a little deeper, to try and flesh out the characters I was beginning to know. In the London University library I found Julian Bell's collected letters and poems, and also came across a photograph taken of him in Spain. In this last image of him, he is standing in a group of people, leaning against the ambulance, wearing a battle helmet and long boots. There is something ghost-like about his appearance. Just as Woolf noted in her diary, this cocky young nephew of hers had come back from China a very different man. 'Julian [has] grown a man - I mean vigorous, controlled, as I guess embittered, something to me tragic in the sadness now, his mouth and face much tenser; as if he had been thinking in solitude... I felt him changed.'

Well, we know why that was.

Since no one else had drawn the two halves of this story together, I could no longer resist the challenge of being the person to write K. That was in the summer of 1998.

Of course, my researches were by no means exhaustive - I was, after all, aiming to write a novel not a biography. It was my prerogative as a novelist to use my imagination in developing the story from its historical basis, and my tale does not claim to be a factual account of the lives of the two lovers.

With the encouragement of the editor of the Chinese journal *Literary Issues*, I have re-read *K* bearing in mind some questions raised by both friends and critics.

The first of these is: 'Was China really that poor?' I am always being asked this question, and most often by people who have read my previous book *Daughter of the River*. What readers of *K* want to know is whether life in China was really that hedonistic. These two questions cancel each other out. This country is so big and so complex that even in the twentieth century there were many different Chinas. Of course, Chinese people enjoyed life, especially in the first half of the thirties, a time when prospects for modernizing the country seemed hopeful. An American critic writing in the *Washington Post* once took me to task with the question: 'Why are books about China always so miserable?' I hope that *K* will persuade him otherwise.

The next question is usually this: are Oriental women really so irresistibly seductive? Are Western men so selfish and arrogant? Questions like this imply a degree of stereotyping, of precisely the kind that was Julian's downfall: he believed that Oriental women were all docile sweetness, while Western men were brave and strong. It was only much later that he discovered that each and every one of us is an individual made up of a mass of contradictions. K was a modern intellectual, at the same time as being a mysterious Oriental woman, and she was also an expert in the Daoist Art of Love. What label, therefore, should we put on her? Is she stereotypical? Are all Chinese women so passionate, so sexual? My only answer to that is to say, once again, that K does not represent a typical Chinese, or indeed Oriental, woman, and anyone trying to use the novel as a guide to Eastern romance is seriously deluded. If there is any message that emerges from this book, it is that stereotypes are not only foolish but can actually prove a snare for those who propagate them.

The third and perhaps most asked question remains: 'Is this novel too erotic?' I don't think that fiction can be more erotic than what we experience in our own lives. Just try to write down the sensation of your finger being burned by a match, and words quickly fail you. If the reader finds *K* erotic then my writing has achieved its intended effect. What I am actually trying to express in this novel is the idea that sex and love are inseparable. Julian considered himself an experienced lover and believed he could have sex without love. He applied this approach to his relationship with K, only to realize - too late, alas - that he had fallen deeply and irretrievably in love with her. A love so erotically charged is a once-in-a-lifetime experience – one for which, in the novel, he expresses gratitude as he lies dying.

So, to those readers who see the erotic in *K*, I congratulate you on your luck: if, when you read it, my novel arouses passionate feelings in you, then how much more will you cherish your real lover? And you will have *K* to thank for that.

Hong Ying

K: The Art of Love

Chapter One

On July 6th, 1937 the Republican Army launched the battle of Brunete in an attempt to lift the siege of Madrid. Several International Brigades threw themselves into the assault and suffered heavy casualties: more than a hundred German planes provided air support for the enemy. As the battle extended into mid-July even the wounded became a target: the Fascist pilots repeatedly struck at ambulances despite the huge red cross painted on top of them.

He had managed to escape the bombardment several times.

On the morning of the 18th he drove a ramshackle ambulance – a truck that had just been repaired – to the front again. On his way he heard one of the Messerschmidts screaming overhead. The road was too narrow to zigzag, and the fields on either side were level scrub with no cover.

He listened carefully to the howling of the plane. As it screamed towards him he stamped on the accelerator, sending the truck lurching over the stony ground. At the moment the Messerschmidt tore out of its dive he slammed on the brakes and cowered under the dashboard, protecting himself from what was surely coming.

The full force of the bomb blast caught the ambulance and nearly overturned it. There was the groan of bolts tearing out of metal as the bonnet of the truck split apart. A tinny ping, then the gurgle of oil. The shriek of steam escaping from the water tank.

The Messerschmidt whined away from them, and he crept cautiously into the open. Broken glass fell from his hair and clothes as he brushed himself down, swearing ferociously. Inside the ambulance the wounded were screaming with pain.

He looked up at the sky. If he had wanted he could have been in Madrid today, at a conference of World Writers Against Fascism; they had invited him to speak as a 'poet in combat'. He had rejected the idea immediately: ambulance drivers were in short supply; and what more powerful poetry could there be than action amidst the shelling?

The truck would have to be abandoned – it was too far gone. When another ambulance came along the road he flagged it down and helped transfer the wounded he had been carrying.

As soon as he reached the hospital he found another vehicle and made his way back to the front line.

This time his luck ran out. On the same narrow road that he had travelled earlier in the day another bomb tumbled out of the sky directly above him. The driver's cabin peeled open then erupted, flipping him out through a wall of fire onto the grass.

★

When he was carried on a stretcher into the hospital of the British medical team, he was covered in blood and dust from head to foot. The doctor who hurriedly examined him found a large piece of shrapnel lodged deep in his chest. An operation to extract it could only add to his pain and hasten his death. There were so many wounded. The doctor turned away to others whom he could help.

The nurse assigned to the hopeless cases approached his stretcher. In an attempt to ease his last moments she dipped a fragment of gauze into a bowl beside her and wiped his cheeks and forehead. His face, protected by his helmet, bore not a single scratch. His skin was pale as alabaster. He lay as if in an exhausted sleep.

She was about to leave when she saw his lips move – he was trying to say something. His eyelids fluttered in a vain attempt to open. She bent down to listen. Amid the surrounding din she had to lower her head until her ear was brushing his lips, but his words were clear.

'All my life I wanted two things – to have a beautiful mistress and to see action. I've done both. I'm content.'

The nurse was astonished. She straightened up, gauze and bowl still cradled in one hand, and looked down at the patient. His gaping wound still oozed blood, which dripped onto the floor, yet he did not seem to be in pain. Having spoken, he lay apparently at peace. It was unusual for a dying man to speak with such self-satisfied composure, but this was a war and anything was possible in war.

He was murmuring something now in a language that might have been Latin – it was impossible to tell. After a while even those words trailed off as he sank into a coma.

That night he was buried in Fuen Carral, along with the others who had died that day.

*

The director of the hospital stripped off his blood-bespattered gloves, washed his face and sat down to sign death certificates. It was the last task he performed every day, and his hand hurried across the sheets. He could hardly keep his eyes open. He signed the last one and was tidying the stack of papers when suddenly he became aware that one of the names he had seen was familiar. He picked through the papers until he found what he was looking for:

JULIAN BELL.
Next of kin: Mrs Vanessa Bell, Mother.
Address: 46 Gordon Square, Bloomsbury, London.

The doctor smoothed out the certificate on his table and rubbed his eyes. He called to the nurse to bring him the dead driver's belongings. He pulled everything out of the bag: the usual stuff. There was something else as well. A notebook. The doctor opened it. The pages were covered with lines – they could have been poems – in a script that meant nothing to him. But there were a few pages of a letter, carefully folded and tucked inside without an envelope. The handwriting was immaculate:

> This letter is to be given to my mother Vanessa Bell in the case of my catching a fatal disease or being killed in an accident, or if there is news or a well-authenticated rumour that I am involved in revolutionary activities.

Good. The man had remembered to leave a will. It made things so much simpler for all concerned. He glanced at the rest of the page. There was a lot of it and no time to read more – he was too tired, and anyway it wasn't his business. He took in only the place and time of writing:

On board *Fushimi Maru* arriving in Shanghai
September 26th, 1935

Two years ago? And in China? What kind of will was this? Snapping the book shut he let it fall onto the table. It landed softly on a yellow handkerchief of shimmering silk, wonderfully smooth in the half-light, with a delicate pattern of bamboo leaves. There was a letter 'K' in one corner, apparently hand-embroidered, in a darker yellow thread.

The doctor sighed. Every one of a dead man's belongings told a different story and, once their owner was dead and buried, each left the same bitter aftertaste.

He shoved everything back into the satchel, stacked the death certificates in a pile once again and placed them in the centre of his desk. His secretary would deal with them in the morning. He stood up, suddenly overwhelmed with fatigue, and moved over to his bed. Just then he remembered that he had seen the dead man.

It was a couple of years earlier. He had been to some sort of public debate in London — he had forgotten exactly what, something to do with stopping the spread of Fascism. Virginia Woolf and Vanessa Bell, the famous sisters, had been there, and a young man sitting between them: tall, ginger-haired, handsome, with an exuberant laugh. He was apparently mocking Professor Harold Laski, who had been defending Labour's European policy on the platform. The young man cracked a joke, and the two sisters laughed and leaned towards him protectively.

'That's Julian Bell,' a friend of the doctor's whispered. 'You know. King's College, Cambridge, making a name for himself as a younger-generation Bloomsbury poet.' There was another eruption from the little group. 'What arrogance!' hissed his friend. To the doctor, on the other hand, the young man had seemed rather like an overgrown schoolboy, the pet of his mother and aunt, and he felt a sneaking envy for him.

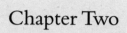

Chapter Two

The only way to cross the Yangtze from Hankou to Wuchang on the south bank was by ferry.

Julian swayed down the flimsy gangplank, and as soon as his foot touched the ground a rickshaw pulled up in front of him, blocking his way. There was a long burst of Chinese mingled with scraps of English, but only two words made any sense: 'Please, sir.' Julian stared. The boy was young, with a pleasant, open face. But the rickshaw squealed accusingly as he climbed aboard. Its bending boards were not designed for him.

Then the effort of pulling began – the boy's skinny body was so tubercular-looking Julian immediately wanted to jump back down into the street again. How could he let himself be pulled along by this sickly child? He felt like a cartoon imperialist! But then he heard the disappointed shouts of other coolies – and his own young man yelling cheerfully back. There was no choice: he could not turn this boy down. He settled into his seat.

The huge urban sprawl of Wuhan was divided into three cities, Hankou, Hanyang and Wuchang, which were situated at the point where the Han River flowed into the Yangtze. Yet Julian had never heard of this colossal city before he accepted the job that had brought him here.

The boy quickened his pace, working his way towards the university. Shops appeared on either side of them now, windowless, with simple counters almost close enough to touch. In one pig's legs and strips of dried meat hung – and behind them gaudily decorated gods glowed jewel-like in the darkness. A pot-bellied male Buddha with a huge grin; a goddess with an elaborately coiled hairdo. The streets teemed with people, some in traditional Chinese gowns, some in Western dress, others in a combination of the two. True, there were beggars, but he felt he had seen more poverty in London's East End.

Julian thought with a certain sense of shame that he had already ceased to be aware of the efforts of his young rickshaw puller. They were accelerating again now, catching up with a Western-style brass band, with a loud drum, playing a tune he didn't recognize. Then he saw young men carrying a sedan covered in red brocade. A Chinese phoenix wobbled on top, outlined with coloured bulbs and, strangely, large mirrors, which swung on three sides, reflecting the crowd on the street.

Maybe the rickshaw boy was curious too, or maybe he wanted to show off his passenger, because he drew closer to the sedan. As they came alongside it, Julian glanced into one of the mirrors and saw his own trembling reflection – a stranger with ludicrous ginger hair, a big nose and sunken eyes. A voice behind them shouted something, clearly at his expense, and a current of laughter swept through the crowded street.

He hadn't thought that he would stand out so much – he had come across a number of Westerners on his way through Hong Kong, Shanghai, Nanjing and Hankou, so they were no curiosity. Then he realized that the crowd was in fact laughing at his distorted reflection, rather than at him, so he joined in the fun, shouting out, 'Hey, you, monster!' and pulling a face. The clamour and vitality of these streets made him suddenly exhilarated.

Then the rickshaw boy shouted something too: *'Maizi bucuo!'* and passers-by took up the shout. Julian could make nothing of it, but he understood what their gestures meant – arms raised and thumbs up. Obviously they were admiring the bride inside the sedan, who had just now lifted a corner flap of her brocade to peep out into the street.

'Maizi bucuo,' the rickshaw boy shouted again, drawing closer to her. But when Julian's eyes locked with the girl's he could not see why anyone thought she might be beautiful. She was very

young, with a prim little mouth. Rouge covered her cheeks in a thick paste, and the grotesque quantity of jewellery piled in her hair made her look like a character from *The Mikado*.

'*Maizi bucuo!*' Pretty woman. The words came again, and Julian smiled. He had already noticed the doll-like prettiness of some of the Chinese women. Now that he was close to the end of his journey, it occurred to him that a romantic interlude in this strange and exotic land might be a very pleasant prospect. Hitherto he had been preoccupied with work – with *The Proletariat and Poetry, an Open Letter to C. Day Lewis* of all things, which he had promised to send back to London. Burying himself in his writing, he had barely even noticed that he was leaving the West. In fact, it was only as the ship rounded India that he realized he really should try and learn some Chinese. A fellow passenger, a businessman from Hong Kong, had come to his rescue, agreeing to teach him Mandarin for an hour a day. By the time they made landfall he knew almost two hundred characters, and had learned a handful of everyday phrases.

Without warning, the rickshaw boy abruptly veered off from the wedding party and plunged into a side street. Everything was immediately calmer. Fallen chrysanthemum petals carpeted the surface of the road. The sweet scent of osmanthus filled the air. Julian vaguely remembered that during these October days there was a festival in China when people went into the hills to pick chrysanthemums and drink wine to honour their dead relatives and friends. He squinted upwards. Beyond a drift of cirrus clouds the blue dome of the sky still looked sullen with heat.

As they neared the university the tree-lined streets became noticeably cleaner. But not even this change prepared him for his new house. By comparison with the houses they had just passed it was palatial: two stories, detached, modern and surrounded by its own garden. The neighbouring houses were similarly spacious, and covered most of the eastern slope of the Luojia Hill. Apparently every professor in the university had a house as good as this – it was extraordinary.

Before leaving Hankou, Julian had made a telephone call to Professor Cheng, the dean of the School of Arts, telling him what time he expected to arrive. Now, as he paid off the rickshaw boy, he found Cheng before him. The dean was bespectacled and wore a long robe, like most Chinese intellectuals. His English was almost too perfect, so that it sounded a little stilted. After welcoming Julian briefly he handed him over to two servants who had been awaiting him for some time and now emerged to carry his baggage. He excused himself, saying that he had other business to attend to but would see him that night at the departmental dinner arranged to welcome him.

Julian followed the servants into his new house. Inside he inspected it carefully. The place was immaculate and fully furnished – the carpets brushed, the fireplaces swept, the couches covered in carefully arranged lengths of embroidered cotton. There were even potted plants gleaming here and there, their earth dark with recent watering. The only thing he did not like was the extreme blank whiteness of the walls and ceilings – it made him smile to himself, thinking what his mother, who delighted in highly decorated surfaces, would have made of such simplicity. His smile broadened. Even if it did start to get on his nerves he only had to look outside for a moment. Beyond a sloping length of mown grass the vast expanse of the East Lake shifted its colours in the last of the daylight: gold, yellow ochre, midnight blue: a faultless, almost Mediterranean setting.

Julian roused himself: his bath was ready. It was all very hard to take in, he thought. He was going to be more comfortably off here than he had ever been in his life before. In fact, when he had first been contacted by the Deputy Minister of Education he had been frankly amazed by the size of his salary. As a freelance he had never managed to earn much, and his family had never been really rich. His Aunt Virginia agonized before buying anything. They had cars, of course, secondhand ones, and his father's parents had some funds squirrelled away somewhere: Clive had expensive hobbies. But the only person among all their friends who had any money was Maynard. Quite a deal of money, judging by the paintings he collected and the support he gave to his wife's ballet people.

Slipping into the bath, Julian began making a rough mental calculation. His salary at the university would be as high as £900, paid in dollars, for teaching nine to twelve hours a week. This was good going, especially since the rent for the house was only $30 for the whole year. Thirty dollars, that is, plus $25 each for the servants, who were expensive because they 'spoke English'. As for his food, that could not possibly come to more than $30 a month. Which meant, he thought, that he had enough to spare for more or less whatever he liked.

It wasn't right, though. It simply wasn't fair that he should be earning more than university teachers in Britain. Maybe the Chinese Government had somehow got wind of his plan and intended turning him into a fat bourgeois? He was luckier than Columbus: he had reached the legendary land of Cathay, and found that the streets were paved with gold.

He clambered out of the bath, wiped a clear space in the mirror and, wrapping himself in a towel, began to shave. His hair was too long; he wondered whether there was a Chinese barber anywhere near who would be able to tackle his curly hair.

★

He heard footsteps on the staircase and there was a knock on the door. What now? The servant stood outside bowing, and without looking at him said that a taxi would call for him at seven. He was sorry to interrupt; he just thought he should remind him.

Julian emerged from the bathroom onto the landing. He was

irritated by the servants. Did he really have to share his house with them? The older one, the housekeeper, was about forty with a large wart on his chin. He spoke almost incomprehensible English, and as for his name – it was completely un-pronounceable. I'll call him Wizard, Julian decided. And the younger one, the one with the piping voice and the rolling eyes, he was a Vole. Vole!

Wizard now told him that the taxi had been Professor Cheng's idea. And now Professor Bell must get dressed; he would call him when the car arrived. He needed time to get ready.

'Get ready?' Julian was puzzled.

'Dress up, sir,' was the reply.

Julian waved the two of them away. What a fusspot, he thought. He lay down on the bed and within a couple of minutes was fast asleep.

★

Julian had smiled at the name of the restaurant – First-Category Fragrance – but when he stepped inside he saw that it had all the luxury of the Dorchester. This was not surprising. There were several thousand Westerners in Wuhan, mostly businessmen who spent their days in offices belonging to the hundred or so companies based in the city, and their nights sampling the best of Chinese and Western entertainment.

Julian was shown to a table divided from the rest of the room by a long screen. Professor Cheng rose to greet him and introduced him to the other guests. They all turned out to be important members of the university faculty – and all spoke English with near-perfect accents; even those just back from Chicago didn't speak with an American accent.

As Julian pulled up his chair he gave a second glance to the women present. There was a middle-aged professor with rather flat features and the nondescript lady wife of someone else from the department. But Cheng's wife – she seemed different. Cheng introduced her as the editor of the *Wuhan Daily Literary Supplement* and as a writer of fiction. She had a quietly self-deprecating manner and, like most of the others round the table, wore little round glasses. Her face flickered as she listened to the conversations breaking and re-forming around her. Her expression was vivid, framed by her black hair, which was tied up in a coil at the back of her head and cut in a neat fringe across her forehead. Whenever she glanced in his direction she smiled, as though conscious of his presence as a special honour.

'I'm Lin,' she said at last. 'I speak Peking Pidgin.'

Julian could not help laughing at the alliteration. Her English was certainly less good than her colleagues', but it sounded delightful for all that, the consonants attractively blurred.

Ever since his undergraduate days in Cambridge, Julian had considered himself an expert on female beauty. So much so that he had decided to grade all his friends' women according to their looks; it was a sign of his authority that he had not been resented for it. Looking at Lin now he couldn't help but grade her in his mind. Her face in repose was nothing special. But when she smiled her top lip curled a little to one side. Julian could not make up his mind whether this asymmetrical smile detracted from or enhanced her looks.

He collected himself and made an effort to join the conversation. Chinese intellectuals, he discovered, knew a surprising amount about contemporary politics and culture back in England, and some had even read recent books. Lytton Strachey's biography of Queen Victoria, for instance, which was apparently being translated by a highly gifted young poet.

Julian had never noticed them back in London, but he realized now that quite a number of Chinese intellectuals had been studying there. Cheng himself had lived in London and Edinburgh, and when he had returned to China he had teamed up with others – some from Britain, some from America – to form a coterie romantically named the New Moon Society. It was self-consciously modelled on the Bloomsbury Group, gathering together poets, novelists, political commentators and architects. There was only one who had been a painter, however – he had studied fine art in America, but had given up painting to write poetry.

Julian was engrossed by these similarities – so much so that he paid scant attention to his surroundings. He did notice, however, that there were dishes placed along the table in front of him, and on each sat gaudy flowers carved from strange fruits and tubers. According to the books he had read during his journey, the Chinese tended to heap food and drink on their guests to show their hospitality, and he had come out tonight prepared for such an onslaught. In fact, no such thing had happened, maybe because most of his fellow diners had spent time in the West. Instead, a modest procession of plates came and went in front of him, each one introduced and described by his eager hosts.

As the meal drew to a close, Julian turned his attention to a Chinese painting hanging on a wall of the restaurant. It showed one man playing a zither and another listening; Cheng explained that it told the story of a local legend that had arisen around a nearby beauty spot between Tortoise Hill and Moon Lake. The man listening was saying to the one playing: 'Your hopes are as high as mountains, but as difficult to grasp as running water.' When the zither player heard this, Cheng explained, he realized that he had met the only person to understand his music, and the two become inseparable friends. Later, when the listener died, the musician smashed his zither to pieces and never played a note of music again.

Julian nodded as Cheng finished speaking. He had come across this story before somewhere, in a book about Chinese painting. It was childish really, he could see that, but at the same time it made him feel he was in a place that treasured understanding. He told himself that it might after all be possible to form a true friendship here and learn to appreciate lives that at first glance were so different from his own.

All the same, these Chinese were markedly different from the Bloomsbury set – for one thing they seemed a good deal gentler and less vain. In contrast, it was virtually impossible for people at home to meet without having an argument of some kind. His mother and his Aunt Virginia would mercilessly refuse to issue a second invitation to anyone that they found a bore or a fool, and, recalling this, Julian's self-belief and sense of apartness were rekindled, and he adopted a similarly critical attitude

Looking around him he said, 'Is this the best that Chinese painters can do?'

To his surprise it was Lin that answered him. 'Certainly not,' she said quickly, adding that the figures were actually quite well drawn – and anyway, no one expected fine art in a restaurant, did they? Even a good one like this. Julian flushed, realizing how rude he must have sounded, and Lin looked away from him. Chinese painting, she went on, aimed to express a 'meaning beyond image'. That is, it suggested the true significance of art could only be found beyond the brushwork.

Julian was intrigued; she seemed to know what she was talking about, and her English became more fluent when she was speaking about things she cared for deeply. A Yuan Dynasty painting she admired, for instance, consisted of nothing more than a few distant peaks above the clouds and a handful of twigs in the foreground. The rest of the painting was empty space. This was Chinese art at its purest.

Emptiness was more significant than its opposite. It seemed an interesting idea, even if he had not fully grasped it yet. There was certainly nothing comparable to it in Western art theory, and he personally knew no painting that had been fashioned according to such principles. Julian bent closer to Lin and told her that he would like to hear more; she smiled at him in reply.

★

It was midnight by the time the taxis had ferried them back to their various houses on the university campus. When Julian reached his front door it opened silently at his touch, but he couldn't find the light switch in the hall and groped around uselessly for a moment. As his eyes grew accustomed to the darkness he saw the couch glowing dimly and decided that he must lie on it for a moment; he had drunk more than he realized.

He thought back over the evening. Cheng obviously knew some of the Bloomsbury people – he had even paid a visit to his Uncle Leonard, looking for advice about how to promote the cooperative movement in China. And now that he came to think of it, hadn't his Aunt Virginia mentioned a visit from some Chinese students, all of them very keen on politics, but unsure which doctrine to subscribe to?

Virginia's name had been mentioned frequently during the evening. Now he was overcome by a sense not so much of homesickness but of great longing. It was first and foremost his mother he thought of, and then of Roger Fry. Roger had died suddenly a year earlier. That was one of the reasons why he had left England. What a pity Roger had never come to China; he would have loved it. Julian had often felt that Roger's admiration of Chinese art was rather overdone, but now he was prepared to admit that the old man was not just an eccentric and might have been justified in his high regard for the Chinese. How he missed him now.

As dinner drew to a close Cheng had mentioned the poet Xu, who had recently died in a plane crash. Apparently he had been the life and soul of the New Moon Society – and before that a student at the LSE and then at King's College, Cambridge, a little while before Julian himself. Roger had taken him under his wing, according to Cheng. Julian shook his head sceptically in the darkness. Who had Xu thought he was? His boasts about his contacts in England were pathetic. Julian shook his head again. It was just as well Xu was dead and stood no chance of crossing his path. Though Lin had obviously thought highly of him.

'*Maizi bucuo!*' 'Pretty woman!' The street cry floated unbidden into his mind, and he said the words aloud. He did not know to whom he was addressing them – to the moon outside the window, or to a woman? He shook his head for a third time, trying to clear the alcohol from his brain, then took up a pen and some writing paper. The air was still; he could hear the waves of the East Lake beating gently on the shore and the wind rustling the branches of the pine trees. Of course he loved women, had loved many of them. But there was only one he really missed: his mother.

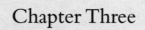

Chapter Three

There was no need to have books sent from England. Although the university had been in existence for just four years, English and Chinese books were plentiful – enough for the course Julian taught at least. The library was built on the hillside and had a gilded roof ridge, which made it look something like an ancient temple. Its two wings were devoted respectively to science and arts.

Before his first lecture, Lin visited Julian at his house. She told him that her husband Cheng had suggested she give him some support in class, since a foreign teacher might find forty-odd Chinese students something of a challenge.

'I want to listen to your lectures on modern English literature, too,' she said.

Her sincerity charmed him, and at his first lecture, as he described the contemporary literary scene for the students, he felt as if there was only one person in the room, sitting there with her dark eyes fastened on his. How thoughtful those eyes were, but how humorous and appreciative too.

Julian recalled his Cambridge days when, arguing with women students in seminars, he had sometimes simply forgotten the teacher. This time he could forget the other students. They were attentive and respectful, a little too respectful perhaps. However, as it was his first time ever at the podium, the last thing he wanted was students as disputatious as himself. He used to be the great questioner – a heckler, almost – at King's, but that was to impress others. Now, as a teacher, it was his role to impress the students. If they continued to be this polite he would be at a loss to know what they really felt or wanted. Once he started talking about Thomas Hardy, however, he felt them responding. He was a great admirer of Hardy – though lecturing was too dry a way to appreciate him.

Lin attended his lectures regularly and was a good influence: the other students began to prepare conscientiously. Each week Julian asked the secretary's office to type and mimeograph a number of pages. They did so promptly, even though they must have had to work through the evenings to get everything done on time.

In his view – he said in one lecture – Proust would prove to be a true literary immortal, whereas Joyce's *Ulysses* was pretentious and a million miles from being a masterpiece. Afterwards, some students came up to him with polite questions. Lin stood at the back of the room, waiting patiently until he was ready to leave. He suddenly noticed how much she looked like the other students – her face, with glasses but no make-up, her figure, her pale-blue blouse and skirt. Yet at thirty-five she was almost double their age! In the West if you were of an age to be a mother you looked like a mother.

She complimented him. 'You certainly know how to give a good lecture – you really make the authors come alive.'

'Every writer is a living person,' said Julian. 'Every poem, every story, is a tiny autobiography.'

Lin turned round to face him. 'That's well said! Very perceptive.'

Julian laughed. 'I was only quoting someone. But when are you going to show me your writing?'

'Why?' she challenged him. 'You want to see my life? Or you want me to see your life?'

It was fun to talk with her: she was so quick that he felt invigorated by their conversation. She smiled again. 'Can I come to your other classes too? English composition, for instance? I want to learn to write in English. Then you can read my work.'

For a moment Julian did not know what to say. So he would see her every day? In every class? And see her 'homework' too?

'But,' she added, 'I'd rather you didn't keep looking at me.' Without waiting for his reply she turned and walked away, blushing. As she went up a flight of steps, she tossed him a 'bye bye' without glancing round.

Julian was taken aback. Among his fellow students he had had a reputation as a ladies' man and had always enjoyed the pursuit of an attractive 'quarry'. Now Lin seemed to be intent on pre-empting him.

He found a convenient patch of leaf-covered turf, threw himself down on his back and looked up at the sky. Overhead, a thin layer of cloud was beginning to veil the sun. He closed his eyes but still her dazzling smile came to haunt him.

'I'm falling under her spell.' He laughed to himself. 'A Chinese woman! Fortunately, she's not exactly a beauty.'

East Lake was huge, surrounding Luojia Hill in a crescent shape and making Wuhan University look as if it were built on a peninsula. There were wooden yacht piers and paved swimming areas. A tree-lined road skirted the dike that held back the lake waters, where the students could stroll along and read their books. The boys mostly wore gowns and the girls had loose cheongsams and wore their hair cut short. Julian walked with his notes under his arm, thinking that he really ought to buy a gown. A foreigner wearing a Chinese gown would make an amusing photograph to send home to his mother, who would, no doubt, find it most artistic.

The rain had stopped and there was a pale rainbow in the sky. A swathe of flowers covered the hill slopes: a strange silvery species, long-stalked, ranging in colour from white to violet. The leaves on the trees were already yellowing at the edges. There was a kind of maple tree here whose every leaf had a different pattern of yellow-orange spots. The whole hill, and the lake as well, were bathed in warm autumnal colours.

I am extremely lucky, Julian thought. This is a fantastic place;

such a contrast to England with its green lawns and little hills. Although I'm not sure this university at the edge of the world isn't just a little too quiet!

He enjoyed walking out on his own, especially at night when the wild geese could be seen flying across the face of the full moon. Once, he all but fell into a grave, opened up for God knew what reason. In the quiet of the night he could hear the distant temple bells tolling at intervals, and sometimes the cry of a wild cat in the wooded hills.

But a campus as fascinating as this did not fit his pre-conceptions of China, a country that should be a hotbed of revolution. He told himself he must try and stir things up a bit, and the idea amused him. After all, he did not like so much tranquility: it threatened to make the loneliness of living in a foreign country unbearable.

Yes, creating trouble was the only way to make the world feel more vivid. Ever since he was a child that was how he had dealt with life. In the house where mother lived with Duncan and his father there was always a crowd of guests every week-end. Those were the days when he tried to prove himself. He would climb to the rooftop and sit with his legs dangling over the eaves. Mother forbade anyone to make a fuss or pay any attention to the mischief-maker. After a while he would get bored and climb down.

It seemed that there were a number of people who shared his revolutionary sentiments. Not long after the semester started, Julian walked into the classroom to find a hammer and sickle drawn on the blackboard. The students awaited his reaction in silence.

Ah ha, so he had a few Reds in his class! Lin made as if to come up and help him but he signalled to her to stay where she was. He did not rub it out. He calmly began his lecture, writing a list of major names and titles from English literary history, from

Beowulf to Virginia Woolf. Before long the whole blackboard was covered, and the hammer and sickle were wiped away almost imperceptibly.

The Communists in his class apparently regarded him as an imperialist reactionary who needed to be humbled. His composure clearly made an impression, especially on Lin.

★

The Government forces had, it claimed, won victory after victory, and the news of the Red Army's total annihilation had been announced more than once. Rumours flew about, and many of the students were full of revolutionary fervour. But Julian saw clearly how naive he would be to join them in playing at revolution. And besides, this campus was too beautiful. It would be a pity to destroy it. The only disturbance he wanted here was of the romantic sort, when a suitable partner turned up.

Life at the university presented one or two challenges. For instance, he was used to being in shirtsleeves. Living among artists all his life, he prided himself on looking casual. Now he had to dress a little more tidily.

Furthermore, he needed to learn Chinese more thoroughly, to commit at least a couple of hours every day to it. And he must get rid of the old furniture in his house and buy some antique mahogany. He knew that he could not entrust this to the servants and decided to go to Hankou to buy it himself. He needed to buy a shotgun, too, to go hunting in the hills. There would also be time for rowing. He wanted to see how far he could get across this immense lake, whose waters stretched away into the distance to an invisible shoreline. At Cambridge he was a crack canoeist. He could probably scoop any prizes here with ease.

He walked to the lake's edge. It was autumn, and the water level was high, reaching almost to the top of the dike. Some students were swimming. A teacher was watching a few of them trying to teach his ten-year-old daughter how to swim. The little girl grew ever more frightened at their attentions. Julian walked over, and the child's attention was arrested by his blue eyes. Scooping her up, he tossed her into the lake. The girl struggled in the water, limbs flailing, and the bystanders froze in consternation. Julian jumped in and with one hand supported the girl under her stomach. She started to move her arms and legs as she had been taught. He heard applause from the bank. After handing her back to the students he struck out across the lake without even peeling off his clothes.

Earlier that day he had selected a few passages from *To the Lighthouse* to use as teaching material and discovered that he was in fact far from being a qualified scholar. No matter how hard he tried, the students still could not make head or tail of it. He invoked the new critical concept of 'stream of consciousness', but this only had the effect of confusing them further. He quoted some critics' views, which had the effect of making him less sure what he was talking about.

Lin asked him whether he recognized the characters in the novel. Of course he did. He was eighteen when it was published, about to go up to university. He had immediately recognized Mrs Ramsay's eight children as Grandma Julia's, his mother's siblings – the Stephens – just as he also recognized their encounters with love and death. And he knew that what Virginia wanted to say was that art could overcome the encroachments of old age. So he used this understanding in his talk on the novel, and the lecture ended with his students showing as much enthusiasm as their Chinese reserve would allow.

He turned the morning's events over in his mind as he climbed out on top of the dike in his sodden clothes – and was surprised to find a smiling Lin standing in front of him. With her hair again tied into a bun she looked even younger than in the classroom. He said, 'Every woman on campus has her hair cut short. Why is yours different?'

'Oh, I just want to look my age. After all, I am older than them.'

The remark surprised him. He thought that her 'old-fashioned' hairstyle had the opposite effect, taking years off her face. How could he see things so differently to the Chinese, even down to the effect of a hairdo?

Lin went on to say that she had had her hair cut short eighteen years ago, leading the fashion for progressive women. Short hair was a symbol of emancipation. Now she wanted to look more conventional, and anyway, her bun was no trouble to do. It took only a few minutes each morning.

'I think you're starting a new trend,' replied Julian, meeting her eyes. 'It's definitely more attractive, just because it's different.'

'Well, you Westerners are always chasing after novelty.' She smiled and walked away, but stopped and turned back after a few steps. She had forgotten to tell him. She and her husband would like to invite him to a casual dinner, in their home, just the three of them.

He watched her disappear into the woods. He used to take risks with everything. Riding a bike or driving a car, he would go as fast as he could. On this campus what was the greatest risk he could take?

In this autumn of 1935 Julian was finally in the most foreign of foreign countries, far inland in a city surrounded by a hundred lakes. Behind him a vast, shimmering expanse of water; in front of him a road winding up the hillside, with a maze of tracks disappearing into the forest. He stood there in the midst of all this tranquility in the growing dusk. His tall silhouette was clearly etched against a setting sun whose last rays dyed his hair a flame-like gold.

Still in his wet clothes he went home. His servants came up to ask how he would like his supper. He did not answer for a while.

It still bothered him that he had to have these two servants. But as every professor had two servants, at least two, there was no help for it. Of the two Wizard was the spokesman and liked to bustle around efficiently. Vole spoke little but did more. The two of them lived in a room downstairs. They must have felt that the 'foreign devil' disliked them, since when he was at home they tried their best to stay out of sight, in the kitchen or in their own room, or they would find an excuse to go out shopping. Such was the fate of servants all over the world.

'You go ahead with your own supper,' Julian told them, 'I'm going out.'

The sun had already sunk behind the mountains in the west, but its light still lingered on the lake, turning the water a deep red. It took a quarter of an hour to walk along the paved road to the Chengs' but Julian had already discovered a footpath that dipped downhill through the woods. It was slippery, covered with the leafy detritus of many years, and extremely steep. It took him less than ten minutes to make his way there, treading carefully in order not to lose his footing. He realized that he could almost think of the Chengs as neighbours.

When Julian knocked at the door there was no response, so he went around the house to the garden. The dean's house was almost exactly like his own, but his garden was much larger. Unlike an English one there was no fence – the limits were fixed by the owner. It was neatly kept and in full bloom. The flowers filled the air with a perfume so intense it was almost overwhelming. He could not help sneezing. When he looked up, Cheng and Lin were there to greet him.

Julian had not put a jacket on, and his shirt was unbuttoned at the neck. His hair had grown again, and the curls stood up in disarray on his head.

'Only you,' Lin said, 'would come in through the garden, like a burglar.'

Julian spread his hands apologetically. 'Do excuse me. I have come empty-handed.'

Cheng said, 'Please don't mention it. Just make yourself at home. All our friends do.'

The Chengs' house contained quite a collection of antiques, including ceramics and paintings. Even the chairs, he was told, were several hundred years old. The backs and arms were exquisitely carved, the mahogany armrests shiny with use. The set of chairs was an heirloom, Lin said, given to her by her mother on her marriage. She showed him round. The screen, door curtain and lampshade in the bedroom were Japanese style. Lin's study was large, with a big desk and a single tatami. She told him that the two of them had spent some time in Japan and that she had studied there as a girl. She liked Japan even more than Cheng did. She was a night bird, she said, and often worked till dawn. Then she would sleep in her study so as not to disturb Cheng.

So they don't sleep together! Julian's heart gave an involuntary lurch. Then he derided himself for letting his thoughts dwell on the Chengs' sex life, and his face assumed a small self-mocking smile.

Lin escorted him downstairs. She began talking about a change to her usual timetable; she might leave the job as the Editor of the *Wuhan Daily Literary Supplement*, since she had more on now. He guessed that she was referring to his classes.

'What's the matter?' She had noticed that he was deep in thought.

'You have so much to do, and I have far too little,' he said obscurely.

Everything at the Chengs' was neat and tidy. There was a proper distribution of ornaments and open space. It was a house with a woman's touch. Not like the merry disorder of his mother's place. Julian admired a large tapestry in the dining room, depicting a banquet attended by men and women in ancient dress. He liked its mellow tones, its feeling of warmth and gaiety.

Above the mantelpiece was a picture frame, which held a yellowing newspaper cutting. Julian looked more closely at the photograph. It showed a small group of people including Lin, Cheng and, at the centre, a white-bearded Indian man.

'Tagore?'

'Yes, that's right. He was our matchmaker,' said Cheng.

The Bengali poet, who had first made his name in London, had gone on to enjoy a warmer welcome in China than either John Dewey or Bertrand Russell. His collection of poems, *Gitanjali*, had captivated the Chinese. The only Asian to win the Nobel Prize for Literature, said Cheng, he was revered by the New Moon Society, who took their name from one of his works.

So Asians stuck together, thought Julian. Trying to read Tagore's poetry himself, he had felt it lacked intellectual rigour. And the praise which Yeats and Pound bestowed on Tagore somehow had a patronizing air to it.

Lin looked through the gramophone records and said to him, 'You haven't brought any records to China, have you? I'll pick some for you. Take them with you tonight. Music will help you understand our culture.'

It was true he had brought only books. Lin chose a few records for him. Most of them had been bought by Cheng in London: Mozart, Tchaikovsky, Chopin and others. Julian saw some with Chinese characters on the covers and said, 'Chinese records? May I borrow those?'

Cheng replied, 'Your hostess said you could take them. So please just take them. You don't have to borrow them.'

'That's wonderful!' Julian was overjoyed.

Cheng smiled back, but said to Lin in Chinese, 'Why does Julian behave like a child?'

'Well, isn't he a child?' said Lin.

Their Chinese was too fast for Julian, who caught only two

words – his name and 'child'. He asked what they were saying about him, but they looked at each other and laughed. Cheng said that Lin liked the house quiet when she was writing. When they were in Peking a few years ago, it was different. Friends from the New Moon Society came and went all the time, and the gramophone was always on.

Julian felt very comfortable in their house. They were so different from other Chinese he had met, much more open. He no longer felt the sense of unreality he had had since arriving in Wuhan.

Lin showed him the collection of poetry by Xu. The first page of the book carried a photo. Xu was bespectacled, like almost all Chinese intellectuals, and undeniably handsome, though a little effeminate. Julian leafed through the collection. The lines in Chinese were vertical, each of the same length. Since every character in Chinese represented one syllable, surely that meant the poems had the same syllabic rhythm as French poems? But Cheng insisted that the rhythm of modern Chinese poetry, like English poetry, was measured by feet. And he asked Lin to read some aloud.

Every Chinese school student could recite Xu's poems, and Lin was enthusiastic about them, especially one called 'Second Farewell to Cambridge'. She said that if there was any work that could count as a modern classic this was it. And when she recited it the lines sounded sweet even to Julian's ears. He asked whether she could explain it in English – it was about his Alma Mater, after all. Lin knew a good translation and recited this, too, by heart:

Lightly let me leave now,
Lightly as first I came;
Lightly wave farewell
To the western sky aflame.

Golden willow on river path,
A bride in the setting sun:
Her splendour on the stream
In my heart makes ripples run.

It continued in this vein for five more stanzas, until:

Silently I leave now,
Silently as the first day,
With shake of sleeve, to carry
Not a wisp of cloud away.

By the last rhyme Julian could not stifle his laughter any more. What a third-rate Shelley! He was red in the face and, pretending to choke on his wine, retreated to the verandah, coughing and spluttering and praying that he had not offended his hosts.

On his return Lin and Cheng were still talking about Xu. Everything this man had done seemed to be of consuming interest to them!

They said that even the great British Sinologist Arthur Waley had asked for Xu's help while he was still a student in London. Julian knew Waley, who worked in the Oriental Section of the British Museum. He lived near Gordon Square and rode a bike to the British Museum every morning, often meeting Julian on the street. Because Waley was also a Cambridge graduate, and because his speciality – Chinese poetry – was all the rage in Anglo-American poetry circles, he was invited to a Bloomsbury gathering. But his mother and aunt found him a bore and never asked him again. Julian thought it better to say nothing of this.

Xu was a romantic, an admirer of the beauty and talent of Katherine Mansfield. One rainy evening, according to Cheng, he had searched the maze of London streets in an attempt to find her house near Bond Street. After some persistence he was granted a short interview. Mansfield, who was wearing a pale-yellow silk blouse and a scarlet skirt, reminded him of a brilliant tulip. They sat on a blue couch under the gentle glow of the lamp. She was hypnotically beautiful. She asked him whether he could translate Chinese poetry into English, as she was sure that only a Chinese could bring out the Chinese spirit. This was their only meeting, since Mansfield died a month later of TB. When Xu revisited Europe he made a special trip to Fontainebleau to pay his respects at her grave.

'Xu felt that Lin could become the Chinese Mansfield,' said Cheng, who clearly took this as a great compliment to his wife. 'Although I think he went too far there.' He got up to speak to the servants on the verandah.

By now Julian had suffered the poor taste of Chinese intellectuals for long enough. 'Aunt Virginia couldn't stand Katherine Mansfield,' he said slowly. 'She thought she was vulgar and sentimental. Her language was all right, which made her excess of sentiment worse. Virginia said it sticks in the nose like a cheap perfume.' He had not liked his aunt's harsh criticism of a writer who had just died, but now he could not resist repeating her caustic comments, and remarking that it was no wonder Xu had adored her.

Lin had been sitting on a couch beside him. She abruptly rose as if to go out onto the verandah. Julian never paid much attention to other people's feelings. He certainly was not going to mince his words with this particular woman. But she took only two steps before she recovered her composure and turned round. She evidently had great forbearance. Most women he knew did not have this kind of self-control.

She showed him a watercolour hanging on the wall. It was a landscape scene, not particularly good.

'It is my most treasured painting,' she said. 'A gift from Xu, before his death. He must have had a premonition that he would not live much longer. He asked me to keep some personal things. Mostly what he brought back from England. As a token of gratitude he gave me this painting as a gift, saying that it was given to him by Roger Fry.'

Roger! Julian walked closer, and indeed it was in Roger's style. He looked at the signature. No mistake. He said nothing more. At least on some points Xu had not exaggerated his social success in London.

Julian felt sad. As a child he had regarded Roger as his real father and did not understand why he had been kind to the odious Xu. The man was clearly nothing but a social climber, doing the rounds of every noteworthy artist in London.

The maidservant had finished the dinner preparations and came out to ask, 'Madam, on the verandah or inside?'

'Ask the Master.'

Cheng came in from the verandah and suggested they eat inside. The night air was quite cool now. At the table in front of the window they could still enjoy the view.

The mountains and trees loomed darkly against the evening sky. The last rays of sun shone on the lake, reflecting silver under the gathering clouds. In the dusky half-light only the flowers in the dining room looked as bright as before.

In the centre of the table there was a large dish of something charmingly called 'coiled dragon', although it looked like ordinary sweet potato. Lin said that both she and Cheng liked it because it was somehow mysterious. It was a centuries-old recipe, containing both meat and fish prepared so that they were no longer distinguishable. The flesh was minced carefully and wrapped in an egg pancake before being steamed. They sat in a semicircle around the table, with Julian, as the guest, in the middle seat, facing the French window. They began with a glass of German beer. On the table there were two red candles.

The maidservant entered carrying a delicate double-handled jar, like an amphora, filled with a green vegetable soup, which she ladled into three bowls. The vegetables were slightly underdone, retaining their crispness, and the soup was delicious.

'What is this?' Julian asked as he drank. It was really much better than restaurant food and far superior to what his servants cooked. He said he might just have to get rid of them in order to get this soup again.

Cheng looked pleased and said that his wife knew a great deal about the whole range of Chinese cuisine, northern and southern. Lin explained that this was only pea-leaf soup. It was really out of season but there were some peasants locally who planted pea to get the leaves all the year round. The leaf should not be longer than half a finger. The greens were put in a pot to which was added a quantity of clear duck stock, which had been made by the long, slow cooking of a whole duck after which the meat and fat were filtered out. She had chosen it as a special welcoming dish for Julian. He, remembering his manners, gave a slight bow of the head in thanks.

At that moment someone knocked on the door. A servant told them a messenger had arrived from the university president's office for Professor Cheng. Cheng went out and returned after a while with an apology. A group of students had occupied the president's office in protest against the Government's retreat in the face of the latest Japanese aggression. The situation was about to get out of control and the president needed the deans to help calm things down. 'They must have got news of some new Japanese provocation,' Cheng said despairingly. 'But what can we do when even the Government's hands are tied?' He gulped down a few mouthfuls of food and took his leave. Lin, looking anxious, sent the servant too, with instructions to come back and tell her if things turned serious.

The house fell silent. Alone together, Julian and Lin were not at ease in each other's company, though evidently the wine had loosened her tongue a little for, after a hesitation, she swallowed hard and said, 'Julian, why did you make fun of my best friend?'

Best friend! Julian knew she meant the poet Xu. He thought she had forgotten. It seemed her restraint had its limits, although her tone was polite. But he had had enough of courtesies and Oriental niceties. He wanted to put a bomb under Mrs Dean's faultless manners.

'Ah, Mr Xu the poet! Was he good in bed?'

Lin's expression froze. The gratuitous insult stunned her. After a long pause, during which he continued to smile amiably at her, she exploded in broken English. 'How…how? How speak like this? Chinese intellectual never do no thing that sort!' She took off her glasses to wipe beads of sweat from her face with a napkin.

This was the first time he had seen her without glasses. The last thing he had suspected was that she might be beautiful. Her face was delicately flushed, and her anger made her lips look fuller. They were reddened as if with lipstick and very seductive.

In embarrassment she rose to pick up her napkin, which had dropped onto the floor, and for the first time Julian noticed her dress. It was a creamy white silk cheongsam slit to the thighs, close-fitting, not like the baggy cotton cheongsams worn by the students. Her collar was decorated with a fluted edging and ivory buttons. A pin of three tiny sapphires held her bun in place.

Good God, I must have been blind!

He realized that amid this throng of new faces Lin had always stood out; he had always enjoyed her company. This should have awakened him to his feelings. So what had stopped him? Those damned glasses! Now his eyes were opened; he saw that he would have to act on his feelings. From the very first time he met Lin he had been attracted to her, only he had been too blind to see it.

Lin sat very straight and began to pluck some wax from the candlestick. The yellow flame flared up. She sat a little away from Julian behind it, avoiding his gaze, and in the familiar light he felt that he was no longer in a strange country but at home. Lin continued to play the good hostess, pouring him red wine as if nothing had happened. Watching her movements, Julian sensed he had already lost control of events and was being irresistibly drawn towards his destiny. He felt that, at the risk of affronting her, he had to separate her from her dignified persona. Not caring that he might shock her, he returned to the subject.

'Modern educated Chinese don't have affairs then?' he said satirically. 'Obviously their British teachers didn't do much of a job educating them.'

She looked at him with complete incomprehension. So Julian began to tell her about his family, much as though he were telling his students about the lives of famous writers.

When his mother was pregnant with him, he said, his father, Clive Bell, had a relationship with Aunt Virginia. After his birth, Mother took Roger Fry as her lover, encouraging his father to pursue her women friends. Since then Clive had been living with this or that mistress in London or Paris, but Mother always kept a suite of rooms – bedroom, study, sitting room – ready for him at home. She decorated them herself with murals. They still cared for each other as husband and wife. Her life-long companion Duncan Grant, however, was bisexual. When his boyfriends came he slept with them. If not, he slept with Vanessa instead. Julian's sister Angelica was their daughter.

'Did they not quarrel?' Lin found it incredible.

When Vanessa discovered that Clive was having an affair with her sister, she simply said, 'These are the two people I love most, they were, they are, and they always will be.' Julian went on to say that Clive regularly brought his mistresses to the house to meet Nessa and he was also friendly with her lovers. Roger, for instance, had all along been Father's best friend. Father's theory of 'Significant Form' in art was reformulated by Roger and was now called the Bell-Fry theory of modern aesthetics. Nessa and Virginia were the closest of sisters, at the centre of the

Bloomsbury set with their wit and intelligence. You could say it had nothing to do with sex. Or rather that it had everything to do with sex.

There was no vulgar jealousy, no prudishness, in their home, said Julian. Since he was a child he had been used to seeing naked male and female bodies at home, mainly life models for the painters. Duncan loved to paint male models in erotic positions, sometimes a few of them together in acrobatic sexual poses, with Mother watching appreciatively.

He was now talking with real gusto. His family's stand for free love against the prevailing Victorian moral hypocrisy was something to be proud of. Lin could only listen as he recounted the details, although she was clearly embarrassed. Her black hair glistened in the candlelight. With her head lowered she looked down at the tablecloth where there were a pair of ox-horn chopsticks and her glasses. She was agitated, had nowhere to put her hands and moved them from her knees to the table and back again.

'And you. *Maizi bucuo*!' he finished.

She raised her head, blushing in astonishment at hearing this piece of local slang. Once again Julian acted on impulse. He stood up, took two steps to the other side of the table and pulled her to her feet. She put up the smallest struggle, but no real resistance, and he held her close.

His face was against her burning hot cheek. Then his lips brushed slowly over her neck and face to her lips. His hands caressed her waist, her shoulder and then the front of her thin gown, where it covered her breasts. Her nipples were unmistakably hard, and he was instantly aroused. They were both flushed and breathing faster, more urgently.

The room was big and only the area around the table was lit; almost automatically they moved to a corner where it was dimmer. Now her lips were on his; her arms, which had been hanging limply, held him lightly around the waist. Almost unaware of what he was doing he pulled her hand down to touch his cock.

At once she jumped away. She supported herself on the back of the chair and looked at him in panic. 'How can... How can it be?'

Julian was nonplussed. Had he moved too fast? Was it his erection that had frightened her? She was quivering. 'It's not possible!'

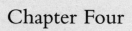

Chapter Four

It was already past ten when Julian woke the next morning. The bedroom door was ajar, and the voices of the servants floated upstairs. Chinese sounded like melodious birdsong when spoken by women, whereas loud men's voices seemed to him more akin to the cries of animals. These servants were talking in the local dialect, quite unlike Lin's soft Peking accent. Anyway, he could not understand a word.

He pulled apart the curtains and the sun dazzled him. He discovered he had slept in his clothes, and they were dreadfully crumpled. At the top of the stairs he looked down and saw Wizard and Vole standing nonplussed before a gramophone with a huge horn.

According to Wizard, Mrs Dean's servant had brought it over for Professor Bell. When the professor left yesterday evening, he had forgotten to instruct the servant to carry it back with him.

Julian got them to bring it upstairs along with a pile of records in a wooden box. At random he picked out one with Chinese characters on the cover and put it on. The twang of the two-stringed Chinese fiddle filled the room. He went into the bathroom, took a bath and put on the underwear and shirt that his servants had washed and ironed. When he came out the fiddle had been joined by the crashing of trumpets and drums. He had no appetite for breakfast – it was almost lunchtime. He threw himself on his bed, reminded by the music of what had happened last night; a tight feeling spread down to his crotch and he had to control the impulse to reach down and unbutton his trousers.

Yesterday evening, just in time to save both of them any further awkwardness, Cheng's servant had returned to report that the situation on campus was no longer serious: the students had dropped their more extreme demands and Cheng had sent him to tell Lin not to worry. Julian had hurriedly said good night and fled. Once home he opened a bottle of Scotch and, observed only by the moon above the dark mountains, proceeded to drink himself into a stupor.

His affairs with women had never given him serious trouble: he would pick and drop lovers as he chose. He never got too involved. His first affair had been in his third year at university. It had cost him several sleepless nights before he managed to get her into bed, but after that it was easy. The reality of sex, he quickly discovered, killed the mystery of romance. After his first experience, the turbulence of his feelings lasted only until he had slept with a woman. One should not, he concluded, let judgement be clouded by hormones.

He was not always so cool-headed, but with each new experience his emotions grew easier to control. The first lasted longest, since it was he who was after the girl. Subsequently the situation was reversed: almost every time it was the girl who fell for him, usually resulting in a storm since the last one had not yet had her exit. But gradually he learned how to manage things discreetly.

His brother Quentin was always secretive about his love life, but Julian's affairs made a huge stir, somehow. He did not set out to make it all public, but that was how it usually ended up.

Sometimes Julian suspected that the reason he grew bored so quickly was not some hereditary promiscuity passed down from his father, but because no woman could stand comparison with his mother. He knew none whose mind or talents equalled hers, nor who were even remotely as attractive. He retained a clear image of her incomparable beauty as a young woman; quite simply, no woman had ever matched her in his affections and perhaps never would.

As always when his mind needed clearing, he sat down to write to Nessa. His letters had always described his love affairs in the frankest detail, to the point that others, should they happen to see them, might find embarrassing. But not him, nor her. Since his first sexual experience he had always told his mother everything. It just happened naturally. She, on her part, took it as a sign of their closeness and was moved by his trust.

He had always been used to the uninhibited talk between his mother, his aunt and their entourage – talk in which generally taboo words like 'intercourse', 'orgasm' and 'erection' were part of normal conversation. The women would discuss sex just as if they were discussing a theatre performance.

Nessa had once described an event that, she said, marked the awakening of Bloomsbury liberalism. It was the year he was born, and she had been quarrelling with Aunt Virginia in the sitting room. They were both upset about Virginia's recent entanglement with Clive. Unnoticed by them, Lytton Strachey walked into the room. He said nothing but pointed to a mark on Nessa's dress and asked, 'Semen?'

They burst out laughing. This single word dissolved all their enmity, acting on their hurt like a balm. Ever since then they had discussed sex and sexual gratification as openly as they did the nature of beauty or of art. They began to live unfettered by social constraints and in accordance with their own needs.

He took up his pen to write to Nessa. He should be telling her about Lin – that he had already had physical contact with her, had felt her full breasts. Yet the words would not come. His feeling for Lin was more than just physical. Am I in love? he wondered. What a joke! He had never really been in love. This damned sentimental Chinese music was making him far too soft.

It took a fortnight for letters to arrive in London via the Siberian Railway, and another fortnight before the reply came. By sea was even slower, though more secure. So he sent two letters to Mother every week, one by land, one by sea. Of course, she never gave him advice on his love life. The most she would say was, 'How interesting,' 'I should be happy to meet the girl,' or even, 'If she is that pretty I might like to use her as a model.' This time, even those words would be of no help.

Yes, he liked Lin. He was trying to seduce her, partly out of curiosity, to find out what it was like to make love to a Chinese woman. That was all.

She was a famous writer with a scholar for a husband, both well known in Chinese intellectual circles. Outwardly her eight-year marriage was successful. Appearance was everything in a marriage, particularly in China. Then what on earth gave him the right to destroy it simply out of sexual curiosity? Even if he married her, he could not give her a better or more satisfying life than she already had. So why should he do it?

If it was only curiosity then he could put a stop to his seduction. There were plenty of bar girls in China to take as mistresses. He felt calmer once he had reached this conclusion.

By now Julian had learned almost three hundred Chinese characters; he could understand more in conversation and speak a few commonly used phrases such as 'this is delicious' and 'that doesn't look good'. He had also learned to use a brush to write the characters with ink, and found them beautiful. The fascination of Chinese characters grew on one, like the subtle beauty of Chinese women.

Julian forced his mind to return to his lectures. He wanted to talk about what was truly modern in literature and, in particular, Bell and Fry's theory of 'Significant Form', but decided that to convince his students that form could be more significant than content was too hard a task at this stage. According to his original plan it was now time for contemporary English poetry. He had brought with him T. S. Eliot's *The Waste Land*, and even Ezra Pound's *Cantos*. But they would be totally incomprehensible to his students. After much consideration he decided on something easier: Eliot's *The Love Song of J. Alfred Prufrock*.

While he was standing on the platform, he glanced over at the seats where the women students usually sat. No Lin. She had already missed several classes.

Who was this Prufrock, he began, this weak and over-sensitive person, confronted by the insignificance of his life and by his fear of wasting it, in terror of his own love?

Let us go then, you and I,
When the evening is spread out against the sky

As Julian started reading the lines aloud he saw Lin walk in on tiptoe, with the mimeographed sheet in her hand. So she must have heard part of his interpretation. Would she begin to wonder whether he was referring to himself, or to her?

Julian was moved by the poem for the first time: it was such a brilliant dissection of the self-torment of a loser. He had never admitted to admiring Eliot, which was natural since he was obsessed by the need to move out of the shadow of such established literary figures, especially his parents' friends. Yet this first published work of Eliot's convinced him that it laid bare the basic predicament that tormented those who lived in civilized society. He felt as if the poem were about him.

'Do I dare to disturb the Universe?' he continued to read, as if he were rehearsing his own thoughts. 'In a minute there is time for decisions and revisions which a minute will reverse.'

He was the 'I', and 'you' was Lin. I already know her, he told himself, or at least I am close to knowing her, but still I do not dare to get closer. Am I one of those middle-class people afraid to reject social convention?

The bell rang, and the students filed out carrying their notes. He saw Lin among them. He rushed to the door but she was nowhere to be seen. Why had he not noted where she was sitting? He had seen her come in. Where was she hiding herself after his confessional analysis of the poem?

He could have caught up with her by running after her along the packed corridors, but stopped himself. As a teacher he had to behave with a little more dignity. He suddenly felt old.

To distract himself Julian took a trip to downtown Hankou, on the other side of the Yangtze River. It was only a twenty-minute bus trip, but he decided to take a taxi. While still some distance from the docks, he saw Vole sitting on a stool on the pavement. He asked the driver to set him down.

Vole was talking to an old man seated on a low bench. It seemed his two servants had worked out some sort of division of labour. Wizard took care of the house while Vole ran the errands. That was none of his concern, but he wanted to know why Vole and the old man were so deep in conversation. The old man looked like a fortune-teller, in a tattered gown and with an untidy grey beard. At his approach they turned their heads to look at him. Vole mumbled something in explanation but the old man stopped him and launched into a lengthy discourse, which clearly had to do with Julian.

Julian asked what the old man was saying but Vole started humming and hawing. Julian persisted. Vole said it was too difficult to translate.

Julian demanded a rough version. He knew that the old man was telling his fortune from his face. So he dug in his pocket and dropped all the coins he had into the bowl at his feet. At this the old man talked even faster, his fists thumping his knee in emphasis. Vole had no choice but to translate.

'Old Gentleman say that you sir a foreigner but very understand a lot.' Vole did his best with his limited English, accompanied by gestures. 'You sir have thick eyebrows, big straight nose. This rich man's face. You sir come from rich family.'

'*Shuo xia qu!*' Julian urged him. 'Go on.'

But Vole subsided into squeaks that sounded less and less like English.

'Your face tight skin. Your ear small lobes. Your frown too deep, you lonely. Not hurt woman. But might…'

'*Hao!* Very good, go on!' Julian encouraged. He was interested in the old man's somewhat unflattering diagnosis.

But now Vole was uncooperative. 'This all Chinese nonsense. You sir must not believe it. You don't believe and they don't affect on you.'

'Why shouldn't I believe it?' Julian said. 'I do!' But his mocking smile betrayed him. After murmuring something incomprehensible Vole fled, at great speed considering the heavy shopping bags on his back. When Julian turned around the old man had slipped away too, together with his stool and bowl of coins. Probably scared of getting into trouble with a foreigner, Julian thought. Well, the old man was leading a dog's life – better stay away from the troubles of others.

The Chinese were bedevilled by superstitions. He remembered that Vole had said to him not long ago that the peach trees in his garden were in bloom again, and he had asked what it meant. Vole had become evasive in the same way, saying it was an omen since it was autumn, but he did not know what to make of it.

If it was not clear, why was Vole so afraid?

This superstitious rubbish was like a disease with ordinary Chinese people, but it did not seem to stop them from making revolutions. He wondered if there was any connection between the two things.

The few bars in the former foreign concessions were the watering holes for Westerners, where news and rumours from Europe circulated freely. But Julian wanted to buy a good desk, like Lin's, so he went to a furniture store first.

He saw an unusual-looking desk as soon as he entered. It was quite big and a peculiar shape – the two ends looked like the stem and stern of a ship – and covered in rose carvings, apart from the flat top. There was also a chair with a very high back in the same carved pattern. The store proprietor told him they belonged to a prince of the Ming Dynasty, and were originally part of a set for a whole house. Most of the set had been destroyed by war and the remaining pieces had been scattered. The proprietor wore a gown made of good quality fabric and spoke intelligible English. The owners of most of the decent stores in Hankou seemed to speak English.

The owner said that the price was ridiculously low for these two pieces because one of the legs on the desk was slightly damaged. But he would repair it without charge. Julian was not sure why he was being so frank, but bought the desk and the chair for only $20. He left his address and the owner promised to deliver them in less than a week.

He was happy with his purchase. Once he shipped it home no doubt Mother would be thrilled. Whether it was genuine Ming or not was of less interest to him than the shape of the desk, which would surely be a great inspiration to the people in the Omega Workshop, which mother and Roger had started. The reddish-black colour of the wood would go well with those nudes that Mother had painted on the wall. Also, the boat shape seemed an appropriate symbol of his ceaseless wanderings.

He went to some other stores and ordered a gown from a tailor who made a huge fuss selecting the fabric and measuring his unusual height. He also bought a pair of vases on which were painted men labouring in the paddy fields and two rich women standing below a tree in full bloom, with smiles on their faces. The ladies were in ancient Chinese dress but their faces bore a striking resemblance to Nessa and Aunt Virginia. He found this astonishing but the proprietor told him that they were porcelains made in the last century with foreign markets in mind.

In the street he was hailed by three fair-haired Europeans, who spoke English with strong guttural accents. They invited him to go with them for a drink. All three were German businessmen. One, wearing glasses, asked Julian whether he had ever been to the Imperial Red House and when he said no laughed at him for wasting his time in Wuhan. According to them, the Red House had the best White Russian girls in China.

The Imperial Red House had a modest facade and was dimly lit inside. It went back a fair way and was subdivided into rooms. It was different from both a French café and an English-style pub. They sat at the bar and were served by Russian girls whose low-cut dresses showed a large expanse of bosom, were fitted tightly at the waist and had skirts ending well above their knees, apparently in imitation of the Berlin barmaids in the film *The Blue Angel*.

Julian ordered some brandy and began to feel at home.

It was only afternoon but the bar was bustling. Westerners greeted each other like old friends whether they knew each other or not.

The German businessmen, seeing that he was a newcomer, began telling him that the prosperity of Wuhan was the achievement of Westerners: most of the quays, railways, hospitals, factories, even most of the better streets, had been built by their businesses. The Chinese, though, were singularly ungrateful for all this and had taken advantage of the Great War to seize back the German and Russian concessions. Eight years ago the British concession had also been attacked, by armed workers in the throes of revolutionary fervour, who had regained control of it – with the ironic result that the Chinese Communist Party could now only use the foreign concessions in Shanghai as their base, where at least they could control their people under rule of law.

'Without us China would be reduced to utter poverty. Most people in Wuhan would lose their jobs and starve.'

Julian did not comment since his handsomely paid job was provided by the Chinese.

The high windows in the bar were covered by thick purple

curtains. There was a hubbub of many languages, and the smell of the liquor made the air stifling.

'How many yellow medals have you collected recently?' asked a pot-bellied Mediterranean fellow.

'Lost count, I'm afraid,' his businessman friend replied in a strong Yorkshire accent. He seemed proud of the fact. 'I've got so much chink totty in my tobacco factory.'

Julian realized they were talking about sleeping with the factory girls. To force himself to remain silent he ordered several brandies. This was far too much alcohol, yet his mind seemed to grow extremely clear as he listened to them boast of ever wilder exploits. The tobacco factory manager bragged of sleeping with five Chinese virgins in one night, raising a loud roar of laughter. Julian was appalled at the crude racism of these colonialists.

A Russian woman, apparently the bar owner, noticed Julian's obvious distaste and said discreetly in his ear, 'You deserve better company, my dear. Come and let me introduce you to Anna.' She was got up in a dress that exposed almost her whole back, she wore too much make-up and she was bedecked in jewellery. The girl she beckoned over, though, was much younger, good-looking, with a muted sadness in her face. 'Anna is Count Vasiliev's daughter,' the Russian said. 'Tango Queen of Hankou. Everyone wants a lesson from her.'

Julian kissed the fingertips of both of the Russian women and said that he was too busy today but would certainly come back another time. He put a tip under his glass and left.

The sun was so bright outside that he had to shut his eyes for a while. When he re-opened them, the houses on the street still looked blurred and distorted, as did the passers-by. He did not know why there were so many people. Before long he found himself walking in a procession of young men and women, obviously students, with placards and little flags. They were shouting slogans.

Julian punched his fist in the air and yelled something too. On the placards he only recognized the word 'Japan'. He did not understand what they were shouting, but whatever it was he was in complete agreement.

Suddenly the orderly demonstration turned to chaos. People in front stopped dead and some started running back towards him. Although there were a few who refused to budge, the streets were emptying, and Julian now saw that in front of them were hundreds of policeman in black uniform, carrying truncheons.

With one yell the policemen charged the crowd.

Now even the most diehard protesters started to flee into the alleys on either side. Julian, however, remained rooted to the spot. When a policeman rushed at him he instinctively raised his hand to protect himself. The wooden truncheon crashed into his head, his eyes blurred, and he fell to the ground.

Julian was confined to bed. He had suffered a head wound and been taken straight to hospital. There was no skull fracture, however, and he was released after the insertion of three stitches. The students who had not run fast enough had been less lucky. Whether wounded or not, they were all arrested and carted off to the police station.

His two servants seemed to realize that it was time to put their minds to looking after him. He was cosseted with delicacies like soya bean milk and steamed small dumplings served with a poached egg soaked in rice wine for breakfast. For lunch he had two dishes plus lotus seed soup. In the afternoon he had a snack of shrimp dumplings. This was followed by a big dinner of fried beef noodles and fresh fish from the East Lake. In order not to disappoint them he ate a little at each meal and asked them to take the rest away. But really he had no appetite and just wanted to be left alone. It was clear that the servants admired him for marching with the students and taking on the police.

The vases and furniture he had bought had been delivered and left downstairs. Only the desk and chair were moved upstairs by the servants. He no longer felt much excitement about these things.

He knew the truth behind his heroism: he had simply been careless and not looked after himself, and been attacked. His wound merely reinforced his low opinion of himself.

It was quite possible that the policeman who hit him had realized that he was a foreigner and although too late to stop the blow had been able to lighten it somewhat. Julian thought that if his wound had needed ten stitches and he had been loaded into the police van, interrogated and forced to answer questions with blood all over his face before being allowed medical treatment then there would have been a kind of equality. As it was, even the bandage on his head looked somehow fake.

He heard someone come upstairs with light rhythmic steps. Julian listened intently. It could not be one of his servants since he had not called. The steps hesitated and stopped. Then there came the knock on his bedroom door.

He did not respond immediately. His heart leaped. It could only be her. He thought he had succeeded in forgetting her. In fact he had been longing to see her, and now she had come.

The door opened.

The first thing he saw was her arm, with a green jade bracelet at the wrist. Her thin fingers rested on the doorknob. Then he saw her feet, in plain blue velvet shoes with a low heel. She was dressed in wide trousers and a short tight-fitting top. Now he saw the whole of her. She looked like a court lady in a painting, her hair in a single plait. He had not imagined that she would take this amount of trouble to impress him, and he was enchanted. Under her fringe she had a high forehead. He loved women with high, open foreheads, like his mother and aunt.

She came to his bedside without speaking. Julian's heart missed a beat and his breathing quickened.

She walked to the window to pull the curtain half across to keep the sun off his bed.

Julian smiled his usual mocking smile, and she gave an answering wry smile. She had learned fast, he was pleased to see. And he instantly felt cheered by her presence.

She sat down on the edge of his bed, looking him up and down. As he watched her face she suddenly rose and went to examine his boat-shaped table. He felt that he saw her eyes moistening.

Somehow he knew that she would stay for quite a while. His injury gave her a perfectly good reason.

She touched his forehead, her fingers circling round the wound, and said in a low voice, 'You've still got a bit of a temperature.'

He wanted to speak but she put her finger first on his lips then on her own, very much like the way Mother used to when she came to say good night. She ordered his servant to bring up a broth of chicken stewed with red dates and watched him drink until it was all gone.

With her close beside him he felt that what he wanted was quite simple, far simpler than he had ever imagined. He felt at peace. After his meal his mind was hazy, and the tension of the last few days finally melted away. Frustration and self-pity were replaced by a comforting drowsiness. He closed his eyes and let himself slide down, down... His breathing became more regular and he fell into a peaceful sleep.

Suddenly he was woken by Lin's raised voice. She was standing at the half-curtained window, very angry.

I must be dreaming, Julian thought. He made an effort and shook himself awake. But it was no dream: she was furious. In her hand were some sheets of paper, which he recognized as his letter to Nessa. Now he remembered: it had been lying on his desk for a few days, since before the demonstration. He had never finished it, so had not put it in an envelope.

Lin asked shakily: 'Who's K?'

69

Julian struggled to support himself on his elbows and half sat up on the bed. 'That is private correspondence. Please don't read it.'

He stopped and saw that his tone of his voice had had no effect on her. He had to answer her question. 'OK, I'll tell you: K is an ordinal number.'

Far from putting the letter back she was still holding it in her hands. She quickly worked it out. 'So, K is number eleven. Your eleventh what? And who is it?'

He had better be straight with her. 'K is you, of course.'

She now looked astonished. She took another quick glance at the letter, at the one line she was interested in, then threw it down on the desk and turned towards him, her voice shaking with anger. 'Me? Your eleventh lover? And I have already had an affair with you?' Her English broke down and she could only manage incomplete phrases. 'You're crazy…! A liar!'

Julian realized how much he had wounded her by writing 'I have already had an affair with K.' Every word of that simple sentence turned a knife in the wound. She was his eleventh lover! At the age of twenty-seven he had already seduced ten women! To her eyes he must be completely immoral.

But worse still was the 'already'.

She was deadly pale. 'I have *already* had an affair with you?'

Julian knew that he was prone to slight dramatization in letters to his mother. But he had only wanted to reassure her that he was happily settled in China. At the time he was writing the letter, he had genuinely thought that it would be the truth by the time the mail arrived in England.

'Come to bed,' he tried, making some space beside him, 'and let's make it "already".' Julian habitually brazened it out when faced with an angry woman.

'You are shameless!' She was yelling.

Julian spoke in a low voice. 'I'm sorry if I have offended you. Believe me, I've never been like this before. But I can't help it, I think of nothing but you.'

Lin picked up her glasses from the desk and looked at him without speaking.

He persisted, with a slight smile. 'Number eleven. Believe me, the last one is the best. Let me prove it to you!'

This was the final outrage for Lin. Looking away, she put on her glasses and left the room. A moment passed. Julian was in a daze. He did not even hear her steps on the stairs or the sound of the door shutting.

After Lin's angry scene his fever receded.

With dusk falling he was staring at the window, trying to order his thoughts. Unexpectedly, she came again, but this time with her husband. She was still in the same outfit, but was wearing a white sweater on top. Once again she had put on the public face of Mrs Dean.

Professor Cheng asked whether he felt better. The wound, he had heard, was not serious. Very fortunate. They brought some Chinese tonic, which they had asked his servants to prepare. 'Just let us know what you need. Give yourself time to get better. Don't think of lectures till your wound is fully recovered. Anyway, the students are on strike again in protest at the violence used by the police.'

Since that was the case, Julian saw no need to offer any explanation of how he had become involved in the demonstration in the first place.

'Please be careful. The University is responsible for your safety,' said Cheng. 'The British consulate in Hankou sent someone over to ask about what had happened to you, to say how sorry they were, as they put it.'

'The consulate!' Julian groaned. He had been trying his best to keep well away from the British consulate and had not let them know he was in Wuhan. He distrusted all government bodies, and what he planned to do after he left the university would certainly not please the powers that be.

The servants pulled up chairs for the two guests to sit by the bed. Lin rose after a while, standing behind the chair. She looked distracted and upset. Presumably her husband had asked her to come, and she'd had no good reason to refuse. Her eyes never left Julian's face, but she would not meet his gaze.

Professor Cheng's ambivalent attitude disgusted Julian. The liberalism that these Chinese intellectuals had learned from the West was half-baked. They would discuss and debate but lacked the guts to put their beliefs into action, political action. He would show them: he could prove himself worth the nine hundred pounds of Chinese people's money that went into his salary.

In Julian's eyes both Cheng's detachment in the face of Japanese aggression and Lin's respectability were incontrovertible proof of the immaturity of Chinese liberalism.

It was soon evident that Lin was trying to keep her distance. But Julian felt anguished if he did not see her even for one day. He knew perfectly well that to go to bed with a Chinese woman meant he must finally marry her. He also believed that his mother would like her very much once she saw her. She would make a good daughter-in-law.

At this point he suddenly remembered a fact that he had never really thought about before: she was thirty-five, eight years older than he.

It was strange. To Western eyes she looked like someone turning twenty, both in face and figure. Compared to Western women she was a little small, with an almost boyish figure. But the youthful bloom of European women was short-lived. He thought back to the women he knew who were around thirty-five. Nearly all had crows' feet at the corner of their eyes, and lips and neck puckered with wrinkles. If they were plump they might have fewer wrinkles, but the fat made their waist and hips shapeless. Even Keynes's ballerina wife was growing heavy.

Well, if a Chinese woman looks younger then she *is* younger.

The true age is an irrelevance: only the form is significant

The fact that Lin was a married woman was not his problem at all. It was her problem, and she should solve it herself. He could only accept whatever decision she made. He did not consider it a moral issue to have an affair with a married woman. On the other hand, if she decided to be his lover and he declined because she was married it was definitely a moral issue – it would be *his* lack of moral courage.

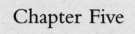

Chapter Five

There was a storm that night, with thunder-rolls that took hold of the clouds and rattled them until every last drop of rain had been shaken onto the earth. The clean, sweet air of the morning was full of the sharp clamour of birdsong.

Julian sat in his garden. He still had a patch of gauze stuck to his forehead, but his colour had greatly improved. He noticed the lion's mane chrysanthemum, startlingly white against the deep-green foliage. The blooms lasted exceptionally well and showed no signs of withering even after two weeks in flower. He rolled up his sleeves and trouser legs and took out a pair of secateurs. He disliked sharing the gardening with the servants – it made it seem too practical an activity – and had sent them away.

Already the plum tree bore tiny fruit. It was odd that the peach tree beside it, as Vole had pointed out, was in bud again. However, he saw that the buds would not open – they were already beginning to yellow and drop off.

He pruned a couple of twigs with his secateurs, causing a shower of raindrops to fall from the upper branches. The scenery of Luojia Hill and East Lake was certainly different from what he was used to – the view might interest Chekhov or Jane Austen, but it was unlikely to have excited Malraux or Faulkner. Nevertheless, he had to acknowledge that it was in tune with his own taste.

In quiet the present passes forever
Down to the sea on the eastward river.
Under the equal grey of the sky
Everything is slipping away.

He was a child of the soggy fields of England. He abhorred the city, London or Hankou. When he started to write poetry he had rejected the 'metropolitan modernity' of Ezra Pound, yet he hesitated to regard himself as a 'nature poet' like Robert Frost, whose work was too loose and too prosaic for him.

He remembered his dream of the night before. He had been running in a field, followed by his brother Quentin. An excited group of dogs charged after them, amid the alarmed shouting of a number of adults. Hedges were knocked down and flowers trampled in the stampede. It could have been either China or England.

He realized he had cut all the budding stems of the peach tree: easily enough to fill the two big vases he had just bought. He suddenly felt exasperated by Vole's superstitious dread of the untimely blossom. Yet if he did not believe it why had he bothered to prune them all?

A sudden feeling that he was no longer alone made him turn his head. Lin was standing behind him.

'I'm sorry,' she said softly, aware of his unwelcoming stance. 'Am I disturbing you?'

Julian did not reply, pushing past her and striding into the house. Without waiting to be invited, Lin followed. In a spurt of anger he dropped the peach twigs on the carpet, heedless of the wet, muddy footsteps he was leaving behind him.

In the bookcases beside the fireplace were quite a few books he had bought in China, and now he leafed through them, concentrating on pretending to read them. Of course he understood nothing, having bought them rather for the fineness of the traditional printing and binding.

Then he looked at Lin in irritation. Why did she not go away? What gave her the right to invade his house? He was irritated by her silence, her stillness. She looked somehow immaterial – like a Chinese painting.

In childhood he had vented his frustrations in tantrums.

Now he spoke to her in a voice that was icy with hostility. 'Have you come here for something in particular, Mrs Cheng, or just to stare?'

Lin continued to look at Julian, her only reaction to straighten her back slightly. She appeared about to say something. Then she turned quickly away, almost tripping over the twigs that littered the carpet, and left, banging the door so heavily behind her that Julian started.

He felt a desperate longing to be doing something, anything. He would take his gun and go shooting. No, he would eat first, he needed food. He shouted for Wizard and Vole, cursing when he remembered that he had sent them away. He began pacing up and down the sitting room like a caged animal. He felt he was going mad, like his poor Aunt Virginia, who veered so often perilously close to insanity.

With an effort, Julian calmed himself. These things happened, he should be philosophical about them. Purposefully he downed some food and picked up his shotgun. Ignoring the mess on the sitting-room floor he put on his cap and boots and opened the door to the garden.

The day had changed. A fine drizzle was falling on the lawn and hunting was clearly out of the question. But what stopped him dead in his tracks was not the weather but the sight of Lin, standing in the middle of the gravel path which led onto the road. She appeared soaked through, and her hair was plastered to her head. She must have been standing there for some time. Just standing in the rain. She spoke with her back still turned to him.

'I can't stay in Wuhan any longer, so near to you,' she said, in a low but clear voice. 'I'm going to Peking. I'll wait for you there.' And without waiting for his response she turned and walked quietly away.

Julian was so taken by surprise he could say nothing. He watched her slim silhouette vanish down the gravel path as the rain fell steadily on his face, his hair and eventually down the back of his neck.

★

The following morning a large envelope was delivered to Julian by Lin's servant; inside he found a novel in manuscript, written in English. An accompanying note told him she had gone to Peking, and had said, as an excuse, that her father was in poor health. She gave him the address and hoped that the novel would help him pass the time on the train.

During the next few days the wound on Julian's head healed completely, leaving no scar. Should he go to her? As the day of his departure approached he wavered. He was afraid of the passion he felt for her and half hoped that he could forget her now that she was gone, or at least get used to being without her.

Yet every time he opened his door he seemed to see her standing there in the rain with her back to him as she had stood that day. He had never met such a passionate woman as Lin; she had touched something deep in the core of his being. He knew that he could not turn down her invitation.

Julian booked his train seat to Peking. Now he felt a different kind of fear. If he had had some doubts why wouldn't she as well? Nothing in his experience had prepared him to interpret the reactions of this Chinese woman. She might have completely changed her mind about him. He might get to Peking and find he had had a wasted journey.

He began his journey north on a Sunday, when the streets were crowded. He and Vole took a rickshaw each to the station at Hankou. Julian was suddenly seized by the certainty that they would miss the train. 'One more dollar, catch the train,' he shouted, leaning forward flourishing a handful of banknotes.

Vole's boy was smarter and saw a chance to dodge the crowd by running on the sidewalk. Julian soon fell far behind. He jumped off his rickshaw, paid the boy and hired another who looked stronger. He arrived at the railway station with only ten minutes to spare. Vole had already left his case in his compartment and was waiting for Julian on the platform.

The train would terminate in Peking, so Julian did not have to worry about where to get off. His first-class ticket had cost him only $6 – a day and a half's wages – and he was so comfortable he might have been on the Paris to Marseilles express. By a happy chance all the notices on the train were in French, and the staff served coffee and croissants.

His new Chinese gown, a beautiful dark-blue silk with camel-hair lining, might look a little theatrical but at least he was snug and warm in it. Fearing that Peking would be even colder he had brought a thick, black overcoat and top hat that lay in the rack above his head. He settled back and relaxed.

*

The train snaked slowly out of Hankou, slicing through a jumble of suburbs and shanty towns, then running through countryside crisscrossed with an endless pattern of fields, lakes, woods and tunnels. They left northern Hubei, and the land flattened into a desolate plain as they drew towards the Yellow River. Centuries ago this had been the cradle of Chinese civilization, one of the places where the world had been formed. Now it looked exhausted and desolate. Everywhere he looked, signs of poverty shocked him: the houses were no more than hovels, barely distinguishable from the animal pens beside them. The people who occasionally looked up from their walk across the fields, gazing expressionlessly at the train, were gaunt and ragged. And the further north he went the worse everything became. Beggars surged towards the carriages as they stopped at each station, shivering and clamorous. At least in England the country retained something of the rural idyll, where life was healthier than for the city workers. Here the situation was reversed: workers in the Chinese slums, though impoverished, seemed to be in a far better position than the peasants, whose misery almost suffocated him.

He was outraged by what he saw, just as he had been by the conditions in the East End of London. The world around him was in the throes of war and revolution...what was he doing here?

Back in Hankou station he had almost stumbled over something as he jumped down from his rickshaw. It was a man kneeling on the ground, supported on a pair of sawn-off crutches, hands outstretched. At a second glance he saw that this ragged beggar was not actually kneeling: he had no legs. In front of him was a piece of cloth with some scrawled words. He hurriedly threw a few coins onto the cloth before running to the train.

Maybe the man had been a soldier, wounded in the struggle against the Japanese? Or more probably a casualty of the Civil War. In any event, neither the government nor anyone else felt responsible for him. Two crude slabs of wood had somehow been tied over the stumps of his legs, and on these he stood.

Julian knew that none of this should have taken him aback. The British press was full of horror stories about life in China, and so were the books written by people who had been to see for themselves. The country was known to be a powder keg, liable to explode into revolution at any moment, but the reality was beyond anything Julian had expected. All he had done so far was to write a 'will' for his mother as his ship had sailed into Shanghai a few months ago.

What seems to me possible is that some train of circumstances may involve me in Chinese revolutionary politics. I have a feeling that I might be a very good man of action, and I want to try this out. If I do anything, it will be from a very firm conviction that I have got to do it. I have a feeling of responsibility about the idiotic and infernal muddle of the world, and also I can sometimes feel an intense sympathy for the poor devils who suffer from it. And if my Chinese friends run risks I may want to feel that I am sharing them.

The letter still lay at the bottom of his suitcase; he had never got around to posting it. During his first weeks in China he had seen almost nothing of the hardships he had read about. Everyone he met seemed more or less happy with their lot. Wuhan bustled with noisy energy and there was no shortage of pleasant places where people could relax after work: even the most modest restaurants were decorated with paintings on the walls and flowers on the table. As for the better-off people – the question of their comfort never arose. Rich landlords could send their children to be educated in Japan or Europe; his academic colleagues enjoyed a comfortable lifestyle, secure in their liberal convictions. The women he had met were, many of them, very attractive, and surrounded themselves with beautiful things.

He had forgotten the other side of Chinese life, or maybe he had unconsciously ignored the filth and degradation.

If his mother had seen the will he had written she would surely understand him and be pleased by the way his thinking had developed. But there was something else he had written, too, something that he was very uneasy about letting her see:

I have had an extraordinarily happy and complete life, and would rather be killed violently than die any other way: of course I should hate to miss the future, and feel like struggling with all my force not to get killed – I'm not a martyr at all – but I could contemplate such an end with considerable equanimity.

If I do anything of this kind I shall take the precaution of carrying cyanide, so don't worry about any incidental horrors.

Well, he did not need to justify enjoying himself once in a while. When the moment came, when the chance to prove himself arrived, he would keep faith with his ideals; he knew he would.

'I will wait for you in Peking.' That was what Lin had said.

He stood up, took her manuscript from his suitcase and settled himself to read. The train was crossing a long bridge, the wheels clanking laboriously and the carriages gently swaying.

Smoothing the first page he realized that dusk had begun to fall while he had been lost in his daydream, and as he glanced outside once more, he saw the reflection of his own face watching him from the twilight. He switched on the lamp above his seat. The table in front of him held beer, fruit and appetizing French-style snacks. The luxurious comfort of the first-class carriage enveloped him like a mantle and shut out the uncomfortable reality of the outside world.

Lin's handwriting was fluent, and although he began by making small corrections to her English as he went along the story soon engrossed him so completely that he laid down his pen.

*

It was about a young girl growing up in a large family. The head of the family, the father, had a wife and eight concubines. Her mother, who came from one of the richest families in Canton, was the fourth of these. The father had been sent there as an Imperial Envoy, and had met her at a banquet where she had helped to show him rolls of precious calligraphy and painting. She wore a crimson silk blouse and trousers, and her delicate hands, like lotus flowers, displayed the ancient manuscripts. The father had instantly lost his heart to her, and, although the girl was twenty-five years younger than him, he had arranged for a matchmaker to be sent to her house that same evening. It turned out that the girl was an adopted child, so there was no disgrace for her in becoming the fourth concubine of the Imperial Envoy.

The father became more and more obsessed with this concubine, and spent more nights with her than all his other consorts put together. Inevitably this sparked jealousies and squabbles, and, even as a child, their daughter was aware that the house was full of enemies.

As an Imperial Academician, the father had a huge mansion in Peking. The girl was constantly getting lost in the maze of courts and compounds. In fact, although born there, she never really felt she fitted in. She had to refer to the First Wife as 'Mother' and to her own mother as 'Fourth Aunt'. When allowed to wander through the mansion she was bewildered by the comings and goings of chefs, gardeners, secretaries, tailors and other assorted servants.

So far, Julian thought, he had been reading nothing more than a tale of a large Chinese family: exotic and charming, but of no great significance. Then everything changed. Writing in terse, efficient sentences, Lin described how the father had been leaning towards the Reformist cause, and when his faction was defeated by more conservative courtiers he was put on a blacklist. While his friends were sent to the execution grounds, his property was confiscated and he was exiled to the desert of Chinese Turkestan. No one except the fourth concubine, the girl's mother, offered to go with him. It was exactly what the father wanted – but even this pleasure was denied him. On the long, hard journey into exile both the girl's parents died.

Even before his body was cold the rest of the family started fighting for possession of what little remained to them. Eventually the compound was sold and the family scattered. The girl was left entirely alone in the world.

Julian read the story straight through, and when he finished the final page and looked at his watch he saw that it was almost midnight. He tidied the manuscript on his knee and stared out into the darkness again. This was not his kind of thing, really, and not like anything he was familiar with: a peculiar mixture of realism and sentiment. All the same, it had gripped him – partly because he supposed that it was Lin's own story. And it was certainly well written: her English on the page was much more confident than when she spoke. That over-rated poet, Xu, the one that had been killed in the plane crash, had been quite wrong to declare her China's Katherine Mansfield – that was absurd. Julian was relieved, and even proud of her. He enjoyed the company of women who had brains as well as beauty, and became more curious about the protagonist and author of the story.

★

He gave the taxi driver Lin's address and got out when he was told to. The driver rumbled off leaving him in front of a tall gate with his suitcase in one hand and his black overcoat folded over his arm.

The mansion dwarfed the other houses in the street. At the top of five steps, flanked by stone lions, stood a massive red double gate studded with gilt nails. On each side a door knocker hung from the fangs of a bronze gargoyle. Julian gave a single loud rap and when the gatekeeper emerged from the gloom he announced himself as 'Professor Bell'. The keeper withdrew then reappeared after a few minutes and took Julian's suitcase. Still in silence, Julian followed him inside, walking first through a courtyard, then two more gates, then around a screen covered with elaborate carvings in front of which were giant urns filled with flowering chrysanthemums.

Beyond the screen were yet more hallways and gardens, rockeries and courtyards. Some were well tended, others somewhat dilapidated. There were plum trees, branches laden with pink and white blossom, their ancient trunks covered in heavy lichen. Cobbled footpaths wound round ornamental ponds. Ilex hedges blocked a direct view through any of the windows, but even so he could hear footsteps pattering along corridors – most probably servants. Whenever one of them emerged into view they showed no surprise at seeing a Westerner.

Eventually the gatekeeper led him down a dark corridor, set down the suitcase and disappeared with the words, 'The mistress will be here shortly.' As Julian waited his eyes wandered over two red lacquer stools placed nearby and, on a plaque mounted above them, four large characters in cursive script. Then, as he lowered his eyes, he saw Lin, standing there beneath the plaque. She was wearing a lavish crimson dress that sparkled with silver stitching and was hemmed with a deep purple band; in one hand hung the silvery pelt of a fox-fur coat. Her hair was drawn into a thick coil on the top of her head and a shiny black fringe hung over her forehead.

Julian was struck dumb; she was barely recognizable: the correct and proper intellectual of Wuhan had vanished without a trace. In the silence they gazed at each other unsmiling. It was as if, simply by meeting like this, they had committed themselves to something they were too late to stop.

Lin spoke at last. Throwing on her coat, she told him that she had booked a room in a hotel. Then she set off down the corridor. Julian followed, suitcase in hand.

On their way out an old man emerged from a large rockery. His hair and beard were entirely white, but his face shone with health. He strolled over, laughing sociably as he hailed them, and introduced himself, in passable English, as Lin's father. Would Julian like to join his two Japanese guests, who had come to admire the flowering plum in full bloom? He indicated two men sitting in the shade of the tree being served tea by smartly dressed maids.

Taking his cue from Lin, Julian politely declined. Lin added that Julian was a colleague from the university in Wuhan, who was only passing through Peking briefly and had a busy schedule. Her father bowed again and returned to his other guests.

Julian and Lin turned back towards the gate. 'How much of that story you gave me is taken from your life?' he asked her with a curiosity he could not hide.

'My father was pardoned by the court before going into exile,' Lin replied, not breaking her step. 'He holds no official position in the Republic now.' She paused, then went on. 'But it's true, I really am an orphan. My mother died a few years back.'

'How come your father can speak English?'

'He can speak quite a few languages, in fact, but only simple phrases – greetings and that sort of thing.' She changed tack. 'You saw yourself how well he is – and he's over seventy. In fact, he's planning to take on a new concubine soon – it'll be his fourteenth! So you see, not all my story is true. I put a lot of true things in, but I left more out.'

'Why's that?'

Lin looked sideways at him then quickened her pace without answering.

As they made their way through the network of courtyards the winter sun came and went at dazzling intervals, spilling down the high walls and casting deep shadows. The roof tiles glowed blue-black and gold, and sunlight reflected brilliantly on the ornamental ponds. Charcoal braziers and incense burners smouldered in some rooms, and small red tongues of flame illuminated heavy, dark furniture. The colours and the scents began to merge in Julian's mind with scenes from Lin's novel and what he could piece together of her childhood. It was an extraordinarily strange world, and the impact on his senses almost threatened to overwhelm him.

Lin was walking faster and faster, and Julian gave up trying to talk. When she opened the back gate and stepped onto the street a taxi drew up immediately, and she hurriedly stooped inside, beckoning him to follow.

They drove downtown without speaking, not even daring to look at one another, though each was aware of the other's breathing. They didn't even touch hands, fearing that any contact, however slight, might blow away their self-control. Then the taxi stopped and they were on the pavement. The hotel was grand, in the Western style, Julian noticed. In a dream he followed the porter into the lift, felt it carry them swiftly upwards to the third floor, entered the room before Lin, heard the door closing behind them.

Julian took a few steps across the floor of the large room. He turned and saw Lin leaning against the door, her head tilted back, one hand pressed against her chest. Her eyes were almost closed, her lips slightly open as she was out of breath. She looked faint. He reached out towards her, and in an instant they were in each other's arms.

★

They could not, later, recall how they made it from the door to the bed. They clung together while Julian tried clumsily to undress her. She made some slight attempt to help, and her fox fur coat slid to the floor with a rushing whisper. But the numerous buttons on her dress defeated him, and as he fumbled she slipped out of his grasp.

With his arm around her again, he pushed her frantically back towards the bed and stripped off his own clothes with his free hand. Neither of them made a sound. Lin would not even open her eyes to look at him. Now she was leaning backwards until she could no longer stand. Julian wanted to lay her down but she clung to him more tightly than ever, as if in fear of falling. She took his face between her hands as he kissed her hair and her eyes. Then her hair clasp and shoes dropped with a thud to the floor. She lay passive as he clawed off the last of his clothes and kneeled astride her. Keeping himself tightly under control he unbuttoned her more easily now. Lin seemed desperately shy, covering her burning face with her hands.

He had waited so long to see Lin's naked body – now, at last, he gazed at it. She was perfectly proportioned, and her skin shone with a warm, golden glow, almost as if it were not of flesh and blood. He was amazed to see that she had no trace of hair in her armpits, nor did she have any pubic hair at all. When he eased her legs apart the lips of her vulva opened up to his eyes like two long petals, converging into the whorl of her clitoris.

Julian had never seen a woman's pudenda so nakedly exposed. It looked to him more like a work of art than a real human body. He was sweating profusely, as excited as a boy during his first sexual experience.

He shifted his gaze to her hair on the pillow: it framed her face and shoulders like black silk. His hand began to wander over her, touching lightly and carefully. He was fascinated by her breasts, prominent and full, with a texture like ivory. They seemed to have a sculptural quality finer than any he had ever seen on his mother's life models. And her skin, from her head to her feet, was as smooth as satin. He held her close to him. Lin kept her hands pressed tightly over her face, preventing him from kissing her mouth, but he grasped her right breast in one hand and took her left nipple in his mouth. He let his free hand explore the rest of her body, from her waist to her stomach, hips and legs. As his hand moved to touch her prominent clitoris, she moaned and he found that she was warm and wet. In an ecstasy of delight he pulled her hand away from her face and kissed her full on the mouth.

Then something unforseen happened. His penis, erect up to that moment, began to soften. He was disconcerted. He lay back and tried to calm himself, then took Lin's small, soft hand in his, pulling it between his legs. For the first time Lin's eyes opened, widening as she gazed at his chest and thighs and then at the soft roll of flesh in her hand. Then they shut tight again as if in panic. But, guided by his hand, she caressed his penis till it grew hard again. A drop swelled on its tip. He pulled her to him and reached for her. Suddenly he stifled a cry, pressed down on her and ejaculated uncontrollably.

'I'm so sorry,' he said foolishly as he wiped her thighs with a handkerchief. 'It's been such a long time since...'

The words were anything but tactful, and Lin made no reply. But after a while she half raised herself and encircled his neck with her arms. She cradled his head gently in her hands and they lay side by side, watching each other's eyes. She smiled with great satisfaction, as though a huge hurdle had been overcome. She had done it, she had entered a new phase in her life.

★

The room was deliciously warm. The radiators were fully on, and a log fire was blazing in the fireplace. And the bed was so huge that when he stretched out his arms he could not touch both sides at once. Sunlight shone on the counterpane, filtering through net curtains and illuminating the little ensuite bathroom and dressing room.

Lin was brushing her fingertips over him now and through his curly hair, her black hair tickling his face. She was tracing him, mapping his contours. Where her fingers could not cover him adequately she spread her hand and rubbed him with her open palm. She worked her way especially slowly over the thick hair on his chest and belly, running her hand over it again and again.

When her fingers finally crept down between his legs she hesitated, watchful. She seemed puzzled, as though the man she held was like nothing she had seen before. Julian lay still, watching her. He pulled her towards him. 'What was it that scared you that night we first kissed?' he whispered. 'Did you want me even then?'

She looked away with a silent smile, while with her hand she explored his soft penis. Her forefinger and thumb, he realized, did not quite meet around it. She caressed him over and over again, as if she could not get used to his size and shape. 'Strange,' she whispered. 'So strange for me.'

Julian rolled an arm's length away from her. The longer he lay with her the more beautiful she seemed. The bareness of her cunt, especially, seemed so bold it made a mockery of her sexual diffidence. Especially now that she had crooked one knee, opening herself to him. He thought he had never seen anything so magical. The outer lips of her labia were soft chocolate-brown turning to a pale, newborn pink on the inside.

He felt himself growing stiffly erect again, even though it was not even ten minutes since he had ejaculated. As he pressed the whole length of his body on her and entered her, he felt her trembling. With her eyes tightly closed, and her tense expression, he might have thought she was merely enduring an ordeal. But at the same time she opened her legs to grip him, drawing him, layer upon layer, ever more deeply inside her. He felt a lick of flame, which blazed up until it threatened to take possession of him, indeed of both of them – Lin's face, too, glowed an unearthly pink. His excitement grew in mighty waves, and soon he came lavishly for a second time.

He slumped down beside her. He suddenly became aware that he was hungry. This afternoon he had gone to her house as soon as he arrived in Peking, then straight from there to the hotel. No breakfast, no nothing. He twisted his head, looking for his watch on the side table, but, as if reading his mind, Lin put her hand on his shoulder. 'Let's go and eat,' she said. 'There's a good restaurant downstairs.'

Without answering he got out of bed and quickly dressed, watching out of the corner of his eye as Lin nimbly did up her buttons. He followed obediently as she walked straight past the lift and down the stairs, pulling up the wide collar of her coat so that the glistening white fur framed her face.

Dizzy with happiness they lost their way, but finally found the restaurant, where they were given a table overlooking the street. They sat opposite each other, a vase of begonia between them. Julian turned to the window, which gave him a good view of Peking for the first time. North China lived up to its reputation at this time of year. Below a deep azure sky the yellow-brown pavements of the city were lined with trees, barc-branched now, interspersed here and there with vivid green clumps of bamboo. Further off, beyond a jumble of rickshaws and taxis, a massive, magnificent gatehouse blocked the end of the street, and further away still he could see softly sculptured hills speckled with blue-green pine clumps.

Lin ordered for both of them, then began watching the street as well. Directly opposite them, at the entrance to a shady lane, hawkers were selling barbecued snacks and bunches of golden flowers tied together with straw.

'You look good in your new gown,' she said, smiling, as if noticing it for the first time.

'I do?' He knew she was trying her best not to laugh.

'Except you're too big for it —' She broke off, covering her mouth to stifle a cry and pointing to the window. A camel swayed past, returning their gaze.

'What a wonderful place Peking is!' said Julian. 'More interesting than anywhere else in the world, and full of surprises!'

Lin smiled at his delight. Indeed, Peking had changed her completely. Her reserve had vanished. She was at home here, away from Wuhan. He reached across the table, wanting to squeeze her hand, but as he did so his elbow brushed against a bowl, knocking it onto the floor. She leaned down to catch it and missed. It struck the floor but rolled over onto its side and did not break.

'What a clumsy fool I am,' said Julian. But Lin responded,

'That's good luck. A lucky sign!' Their hands came together and their fingers interlaced.

Julian looked around and felt a spasm of disappointment. What a pity all the tables were separately screened. He felt proud of Lin's beauty and wanted others to see it, too, to see him with her.

Their food came: fried spring rolls, stewed mushrooms, fried bean sprouts, lotus seed soup, bean curd with melon seeds and a hollow gourd filled with shrimps. A profusion of plates covered the table in a medley of tastes, colours and smells. He thought of his father. Clive would enjoy this so much; he really should come to Peking and find a mistress here.

He still held one of Lin's hands in his. What time was it? Three o'clock? Four? This was meant to be lunch and dinner rolled into one, but suddenly he felt no appetite for it. He felt Lin's palms grow moist, and her eyes filled with desire.

'I didn't make you happy up there, my darling, did I?' he said.

There was no answer and Lin looked down at the tablecloth. But she was scratching on his palm with one finger, as though she was writing something. He couldn't work out what it was, but he could guess. His heart began to beat faster.

He put down his chopsticks and reached out to caress her face. Her lips parted and she breathed faster.

'Oh my God,' he said, as if to himself. 'I can't stand it anymore.'

Lin's face flushed and began to bead with sweat. 'I'm going to come just looking at you,' she whispered. Throwing down money onto the table he pulled her to her feet. They wove quickly between the tables and out of the restaurant towards the lift. When they reached their floor she ran ahead of him down the empty passage to their room. He had his coat off before they reached the door. As it shut behind them Lin already had half her buttons undone. When he turned round from locking the door she was naked. She stood on tiptoe and threw her arms around his neck.

Chapter Six

When she had overcome the last of her inhibitions, Lin became a completely different woman. Her face glowed pink. She looked even younger than before, almost like a young graduate who had just discovered a new game.

He felt a twinge of guilt, as if he was violating some taboo, which only excited him further. He was eager to enter her. But Lin was in no hurry. Not until his eyes were hot with desire did she let the tip of his penis slide inside her. Then she heaved her body up, and with each move allowed him to penetrate her more deeply. She was swallowing him bit by bit, till his whole sex was anchored securely within her.

In the midst of this, strange and irrational worries plagued him. Her body seemed so delicate, yet they were meshed so tightly together that he felt his penis was burning through her, almost to her liver or spleen, and he was scared that he might injure her. But her half-closed eyes and deep sighs reassured him.

He held her, and, lying side by side, she reached to kiss him, a kiss so intense that it drew the breath out of him. She gripped his hair with one hand and his shoulder with the other. At the same time, she gradually straightened her legs until their bodies overlapped so that they were indistinguishable from one another. This position made his erection curve and twist inside her so forcefully that they both gasped for breath.

Then she began to moan softly, almost tunefully, as if chanting. He stifled a cry, on the verge of coming, and she responded by gripping him even more tightly. He groaned almost painfully and, with great relief, spurted inside her.

Julian closed his eyes, overwhelmed by fatigue, and began to drift off to sleep. Lin was asleep beside him with one leg draped over his thighs, her arms around his neck. Her face was pressed lightly against his lips. Julian fell into a sweet unconsciousness.

He was a small boy again, in the arms of his mother, who had just lifted him out of the bath, rubbed him dry, kissed him and put him to bed. He had run wild in the fields all day long, and now he sunk into a well-deserved sleep. Suddenly he felt his penis harden. Now it was in a warm wet place. He struggled towards consciousness.

My God, it was his mother!

He started awake in fright. Lin was lying with her leg and arms entwined around him. But his penis was now inside her. She had been cradling him as he slept in such a way that he had only to harden a little for her to hook him into her. She was innocently humming a tune and having sex with him while he slept!

At the sight of his surprised expression, Lin hid her face in his chest in embarrassment. 'You're wonderful! You can sleep and make love at the same time,' she said. The glow of the evening sun shone through the half-drawn curtains. It was nearly night. Was this mad day going to get even crazier?

Her face, her hair and her body were illuminated by the sun's rays. She seemed to glow with energy, intoxicated with their continued lovemaking. Didn't she need to rest? Apparently not. Unlike Julian her vitality and sexual appetite showed no sign of abating.

Seeing his confusion she let him go bit by bit. His glistening shaft appeared inch by inch and began to soften and shrink until only the tip remained inside her. He had never had such passionate sex with a woman before. In fact, he felt as if he had never had sex at all until today. And he had thought her a prudish intellectual, this Chinese Mansfield. Where had this insatiable woman come from?

I'm so tired, he thought. She's killing me. Somehow the

thought pleased him. What a way to go! There can't be many men in the world as lucky as me. He smiled wryly to himself: I might die of a different kind of torture, at least then I'd have no need of cyanide.

His anxieties seemed suddenly ridiculous. Here they were in this most peaceful of Chinese cities, in the gathering dusk, and he was in her arms. Sex with this mysterious, beautiful woman was so good – he relaxed into a half-dreaming state again.

When he finally woke up it was pitch dark. Reaching out his hand he grasped only a handful of the sheet that covered him. He was thrown into a panic. Where was she?

Then he rubbed his eyes and saw the glimmer beneath the dressing-room door, which was closed. He got up and pushed it open. She was already dressed in her red silk cheongsam, and sat doing her hair. She laughed at the sight of him standing stark naked, blinking in the light. He went over to her and bent over to hug and kiss her. 'Here you are.'

Lin said, 'Were you afraid that I had left?'

He did not reply, saying only, 'It's evening, let's go down and have a good meal.' He took a hasty bath and threw on his clothes. He was a little apprehensive that he might end up in bed again if they did not get out of the room fast.

Opposite the hotel they found a Hubei-style restaurant. As the first course was put on the table two waiters carried over a gently slopping fish tank to show them half a dozen blunt-snouted breams – a delicacy of Wuchang – swimming among the waterweeds. Lin ordered the largest one, and the two waiters retreated with bows.

The rice wine, in which a few red wolfberries bobbed, was smooth and dry. Julian drank slowly, not knowing what to say.

'I know you're puzzled,' Lin said. 'I'm different to the woman you thought you knew, aren't I? But I'm not a "nymphomaniac", as you Westerners would say.' She spoke fluently now, as if she was giving a prepared speech of explanation.

Her father was a book collector, she went on, with a superb collection of rare books, some of which existed in only one copy. Her mother had brought to him in her dowry a number of esoteric Daoist scriptures, believed to be long lost. Among them a hand-written version of the *Jade Chamber Classic*, the legendary 'Art of Love', mentioned by bibliographers down the centuries but not previously seen. His fantasy about these books was part of the reason why he valued her mother above any other concubine. It delighted him even more to find out that she was adept in the Daoist self-cultivation techniques described in the book.

So the two set their minds to improving their lovemaking using the book, which was an application of Daoist metaphysics to the erotic arts.

This *Classic* was Lin's father's pride and joy. He quoted the old saying that: 'To buy a good book is the same as to buy a pretty concubine, but its beauty is greater and lasts longer.' Since he had now acquired both a pretty woman and a priceless manuscript he was doubly fortunate.

Lin's mother maintained that her own mother had even more knowledge than the book. The grandmother had learned its precepts by heart and passed them down to her daughter. Before her marriage she had added practical advice to the theory. It had taken exceptional mental agility and a certain natural gift to master the art before her marriage, her mother said.

And she had aptitude. In their daily lovemaking she arrived at a unique mastery of the *Classic* and added her own skills. However, when Lin was a young adult and asked her father to let her have a look at the book he flew into a rage. No one – he hissed – should even have mentioned its existence to their daughter. This book was not on show to anyone, it was the only extant copy, and would remain so.

Father once told her that, in 1927, the well-known book collector in Hunan, Ye Dehui, wrote to him saying that he would crawl all the way to Peking just to have a glimpse of the fabled text. By the time this half-threatening half-joking letter arrived Ye Dehui had already been arrested by the Communists in the south. They executed him as a notorious 'local despot', as an example to other landlords. So Ye would never be able to 'crawl' anywhere, let alone to Peking – to her father's relief. But he felt sorry for him. Ye's mistake was to have published his private collection as *The Chinese Art of Love*. He did not realize that this century was not the time for such stuff. The Communists declared him a criminal for making profits from selling 'feudalistic pornography', and nobody came to his defence.

But Lin's father was also progressive, proud that his daughter was a novelist of the New School. He was anxious to see his daughter forging ahead in the modern world. The Art of Love was his private passion. Such esoteric knowledge had no role in this era of progress, and he did not want it passed down to his daughter. He turned against his favourite concubine, who eventually died three years after Lin's marriage. Lin suspected foul play within the large household but her father refused to let the police carry out an investigation.

Both parents agreed that they had to raise their daughter as a modern woman, and Lin was educated at an expensive girls' boarding school in the British concession in Tianjin. However, when she was a child, whenever they had time to be together, her mother taught her meditation and other Daoist self-cultivation methods. That was why, when the time finally came, Lin had no difficulty in learning the Art of Love.

The whole tale left Julian at a loss to know what to say. When she had discussed modern Chinese literature and culture with him he could follow her arguments and form his own judgements. But the idea of Lin's mother teaching her daughter the 'Art of Love' was unimaginable. His thoughts turned to women lovers he knew: to his Aunt Virginia and her supposed lesbian relationship with Vita Sackville-West – although the truth was far less interesting. Then he remembered having seen the nude photo of his mother taken together with Molly McCarthy. He was five at the time. In those years only prostitutes would allow themselves to be photographed naked. What had made them do it? He recalled how beautiful his mother's body had been.

'Did you have lesbian sex with your mother?' He asked her straight out.

Lin did not answer. Instead, she raised her glass in a toast to Julian. When she blushed her eyes darkened to a steely blue.

Lin sipped the wine. Matchmakers had lain siege to the house as soon as she was fifteen, she said. But her parents agreed that since they wanted her to be a new woman she should be given the right to choose her own husband. When she met Cheng he was a professor at Peking University and she was already a well-known writer. During the 1924 Tagore visit they came to know each other better, but it was not until three years later, when she was twenty-seven, that she accepted his proposal.

But it turned out that the Western-educated Cheng worshipped progress and didn't even want to hear what he called Daoist superstitions, and the Art of Love was, in his view, a symbol of the most degenerate and reactionary aspects of Chinese feudal culture. When she tried it out on him it was a fiasco. He reacted as if he was being poisoned – in fact, it had made him physically ill for weeks.

After that, sex between them was rare and half-hearted. She returned to her old habit of applying the Art to her self-cultivation. Judged by the standards of the new China, their marriage, the liaison of a well-known literary scholar with a famous novelist, was highly successful. Had she told anybody about her true desires they would have thought she was insane.

Today she had had the opportunity to put the theory to its first real test. As she had expected, sex in accordance with the advice given in the *Jade Chamber Classic* had been intensely invigorating.

'But what I have said is not something that should be admitted by an educated modern woman,' she added with some embarrassment.

Julian took her hand; he now understood better her odd ideological dilemma. 'You have a dual personality, isn't that right?'

Lin acknowledged this. She was like two people in one body. To the outside world, a woman of letters with a European-style education; inwardly, a traditionalist adept in an art of life passed down to her by her parents and grandparents. She had never revealed this part of herself to anyone, just as she had never expected to become involved with a European.

'So, you can, er, draw out my "inner energies" during sexual intercourse?' Various scenes from this hectic day flashed before him.

'You're brilliant,' Lin replied with pleasure. 'You don't need much teaching.'

Julian felt the whole thing was scarcely believable. 'You make it sound like a kind of sexual vampirism.'

'So you think I'm sucking your life from you, do you? You have to understand, the Art of Love is a form of mutual nourishment, the joining of yin and yang. Once a man has learned the Art, he benefits too – you remember my father?'

It was true that Lin's father, at over seventy, was as youthful and vigorous as a man not yet fifty, but Julian was not sure he was up to it. If he failed, would he not just be sucked dry? There would be nothing left for Lin but the dregs of his yang energy! On second thoughts, he began to see the funny side of it – here he was, a man, moaning about being reduced to the sex toy of a woman. He had heard enough complaints in his life about men using women as sex objects. Now the boot was on the other foot.

But then again, he thought, surely this was a load of Chinese superstition, entirely unscientific and irrational, though exotic. As for his uncontrollable orgasms, they were purely the effect of his months of abstinence. From now on he would make sure he measured up to this Chinese bluestocking.

Lin looked at him and, interrupting his train of thought, said that her mother had told her there was an imbalance between the sexes: a man's duct is too narrow to draw yin energy easily from a woman, whereas a woman can absorb the yang with all her inside parts. That was why few men could learn the Art. If a man can open up that channel then both sides get the benefit.

'And this evening was wonderful. You didn't ejaculate at all. It is said in the secret book that with one intercourse and no release a man gets stronger; with two, eyes get brighter; with three, no disease is incurable; with four...'

Both of them burst out laughing, and he urged her, 'Go on! Go on!'

'Well let me skip,' Lin said, 'since you don't seem to believe me. With twelve, you become immortal!'

'My God,' Julian said, 'that's worth trying for.' But he knew that in their last session he had simply been too sleepy and had let Lin have her way. When fully awake he was simply not capable of holding back.

'But,' he asked, 'if a man does not come, why on earth does he need sex?'

'In order to make the woman happy, the man always has to remain vigorous. That is said in the ancient Chinese books,' Lin said emphatically.

'So, the purpose of sex is women's pleasure,' Julian marvelled. It was the first time he had heard such unequivocal woman-centred sexology. The male chauvinism in Chinese society seemed to stop at the threshold of the bedroom. Inside, yang had to harmonize itself with yin. Pouring himself another glass of wine he asked directly, 'So then, how many orgasms did you have today?'

'How many? A woman adept in the Art of Love does not count how many.' She was still a little bashful when talking about her own experience. 'Today the whole day was an orgasm for me.' She sighed as if recalling something too good to be true. 'I was floating like a cloud driven higher and higher by the wind – the first time in my life – like an immortal drifting above. But that's enough of that, Julian. Let's just enjoy each other.'

She put down her chopsticks and looked at him with affection in her eyes.

Julian could not help thinking there were few things better in the world than this Chinese Art of Love. Meeting her gaze, he gripped her hand. Yes, he wanted to go on enjoying her, even after this day of exhausting lovemaking; he wanted to finish the meal and take her back upstairs to bed. He could not let go of her hand: the darkness might steal her away. Life was so good in her company. The Art of Love was neither here nor there. So what if he was beaten in the erotic arts by a Chinese woman; he was the first Englishman to be so defeated.

This time both of them were calmer. They undressed without hurry and embraced. It was the middle of the night now, and cooler inside the room, even with the heating on. From time to time Lin tried to cover him with the quilt, but he pushed it back: he needed to have an unimpeded view of her body. For the same reason he insisted on leaving the lights on. He remembered those big-boned women back home, those girls who reached puberty too early and then aged prematurely and grew fat, while Lin was curvy but slender. He could not understand how Oriental women managed to combine both elements in one body.

He felt that now they were very familiar, very intimate with each other. With one glance, one movement or one particular sound they knew what each other wanted.

'So teach me,' he said, 'how not to come.'

Her arms around his neck, Lin said that she did not know, for she was not a man. 'It's called "Reining Back the White Ox". There is advice on how to do it, but if a man can't learn by himself no advice works.' But, she added, if Julian set his mind on learning it it should be easier.

'How do you know?' asked Julian.

'Well, I just have a feeling.' Lin blushed again. 'But today was different. From now on we shall practise together, shan't we? The Daoist classics say that with twelve successes a man even in advanced age can retain his youth.'

'Well, I don't want to live for ever. I want to stop with you, at K!'

Lin laughed. 'It doesn't mean twelve women. It means making love twelve times *every night*!'

Julian thought of Roger Fry, whom he regarded as his spiritual father. While lecturing on the history of fine art at Cambridge, Fry had declared that he wished he could devote the whole term to Chinese art. He was filled with awe by the animal carvings on the bronze vessels of Chou, whose power to impress only seemed to increase with the centuries. Western missionaries never comprehended the Chinese attitude towards evil, which was half serious, half light-hearted, whereas the monstrous horrors in Christianity were never to be laughed at. How was the perfect balance achieved? Was it because the foundry manager and his wife were expected to jump into the molten metal to provide perfect harmony between the yin and yang for casting?

For the art of life, the Chinese are willing to give up life for art. At last he understood Roger's ironic conclusion.

Lin seemed to be laying down a challenge to him. Now you know a little of the Chinese philosophy of sex and a little about the harmonizing of Man and Woman. The same truth applies to art and to humans. Are you willing to jump into the flames with me? Meet yin with yang? Do you dare?

All his life Julian had relished a sexual challenge. His British or French lovers knew only how to say 'I love you' when excited. How unimaginative! Now he had met the Ancient Orient in Lin. His pulse rose in response.

He kissed her over and over. He entered her. With Lin kneeling over him, gripping his sides with her legs, he realized that her breasts changed dramatically when she was aroused. They hung down like Chinese terracotta teacups, the nipples, with their delicate pinky brown tips, protruding like the narrow top of the teacup lid. All his life he had felt as if he was in search of a colour, a colour that he could not put into words. In his mother's studio the walls were covered with countless nudes, yet the colour of the women's nipples was wrong and left him somehow dissatisfied. No longer. With every movement their bodies made, the large haloes around her nipples were suffused with this colour. They glistened with tiny beads of sweat. He sighed and took a nipple in his mouth, where it grew larger. She loved to close her eyes as her desire increased, showing the dark, dense line of her eyelashes. Her ears were delicate and her neck fine and long. He had to stop looking at her or the sight of her face flushed with the elation of her orgasm made it impossible for him to hold back.

She covered his eyes with her hands and bit his ear gently. 'Slow down, hold on,' she said.

But it only aroused him more. Reining Back the White Ox, indeed! How could one possibly do that with this woman!

Almost immediately, his mind cleared. He had always been afraid of the woman getting too serious in a relationship. This lovable creature curled up on his chest just wanted him for sex; she was using him as a sex object. She just needed her fill of yin and yang to keep her young and beautiful. This thought comforted him;

she would not be trying to steal his freedom, it was wonderful!

Her legs clasped him, her body still jerked, and the mousetrap inside her was still clenched, although by now he was going soft. It looked like he would have to sleep for the rest of the night like this.

He had always been scared of the bonds of love, but he realized that Lin had never said the word, not in English nor in Chinese. Even when she climaxed she did not ask if he loved her. Strange, but good. His worries about coming to Peking had been groundless.

Chapter Seven

It was fascinating to walk the streets in the evening. Doorways were hung with banners printed all over with prayers and blessings; many people in the crowd carried lanterns, so the way ahead glittered like moonlight on water, and snatches of their conversation, in a velvety local accent, came and went on the still evening air. Occasionally there were glimpses into the windowless shops – calligraphy strips and paintings, hanging scrolls and brilliant fans. In the south it would be raining and icy cold. Here the air was dry and bright, the evening sky a deep blue as dusk fell. It felt very peaceful

Lin didn't stay in the hotel every night. Often she returned home in the small hours. There were not that many Westerners in the hotel in Peking, and their presence was conspicuous even though it was a hotel run by Westerners; rumours could easily start. It was deepest winter, though, and at least on the streets they could hide their faces behind upturned collars.

Lin also felt uncomfortable around her father's concubines and domestics. Their favourite pastime in the big compound was gossiping. But they knew that she was very highly educated and a famous novelist who had a great deal of contact with the outside world: when she didn't want to go back she could just say she was staying with her friends, though in fact she had to avoid all her friends in Peking.

One afternoon they found themselves in the park which covered Jingshan Hill on the edge of the walled city. The winter sky was a startling clear blue. The city noises faded away; there were few people around. From here they could gaze across the suburbs into the centre. Lin pointed to the hills, explaining how many emperors and princes had built huge tombs there and died with their treasures buried beside them.

'I'd love to see some treasure,' said Julian. 'I'd love to be able to show the people at home. Why don't we go and see if we can find some little thing?'

'Why not?' Lin responded lightly. 'We'll go tonight – we'll make a dream journey.' She was wearing water-blue satin trousers hemmed with silver thread and a yellow silk blouse accentuating her slim waist. In her high boots she looked more like a Manchu court lady than a Chinese woman, especially with her hair piled on top of her head.

She pointed to the crooked branch of a tree growing near where they stood and said the last Ming Emperor had hanged himself from it when a rebel army of peasants had overrun Peking. A black crow perched there now, cawing brokenly. It was just as it should be, Lin said. There were more crows than any other kind of bird in the city during the winter, and if they kept quiet it was a bad omen. Come springtime it was the magpies' turn to be heard, and that, too, augured well for the future.

'What if the crows and magpies make a noise at the same time?' asked Julian.

'They don't.'

'I thought I just heard a magpie.'

Lin said that he must have been mistaken, she had never heard such a thing herself. She led him further up the hill towards a small pavilion. This was the highest point inside the city walls, and when they looked down the grounds of the Imperial Palace looked like a colossal chessboard, with their neat, symmetrical design: the glistening golden roofs, the gates, the squares and walkways stretched away to the southernmost point of Tiananmen, the Gate of Heavenly Peace. To the north-west lay the Summer Palace, a huge garden with a large lake, white marble bridges and glittering buildings.

It was unusually warm this winter, Lin commented. Julian nodded. It was, indeed, not nearly as cold as his books about

Peking had led him to expect, and all the snow had melted. In truth, although he was impressed by the beauty of the natural surroundings, he felt that much of what he could see was more than a trifle vulgar. The various palaces were painted in gaudy colours and their gardens were all excessively elaborate. What other royal family would have emptied the Imperial coffers building the Summer Palace, leaving the navy underfunded? Ultimately it made sense, however, otherwise it would have been money sent straight to the bottom of the sea. Obviously the Imperial opulence had a bad influence on everyone else. Wherever he looked were signs that those who could spent lavishly: gardens full of willows, rooms stuffed with ornate furniture. There seemed to be a national obsession with ostentation, right down to the whole arcane business with concubines. He, by contrast, was satisfied with only one lover: her lovemaking was so inventive it was like having a harem.

Lin slid her hand into his coat pocket. He could feel her happiness, and her pleasure in being alone with him in the park. 'Aren't you cold?' she asked him. He shook his head, but all the same she took off her long woollen scarf and wrapped it round his neck, flipping one end across his chest and letting the other dangle down his back.

In the bright winter sunshine the cold wind had given her rosy cheeks. Even though she was only wearing light make-up she still looked more beautiful than anything he had seen in the city below them. She seemed completely indifferent to the cold, and the breeze pressing lightly against her marked the soft swell of her breasts. He looked around at the clear blue sky, the bare brown trees, the pines, the artfully designed hills, the lawns. He liked Peking much better than Wuhan, especially because she was here with him. He told Lin how he felt.

'Will you use this in your lecture?' she said.

'Will I use what? What lecture?'

'This place; what we're seeing. When you talk about

"empathy". An ancient Chinese poet once wrote: "I saw that the green hills were delightful, and I knew they must see me in the same way." It could have been written especially for you.' Her laughter was infectious.

Julian had never seen her so happy. Really, she was an enchanting woman. So natural, yet sensitive, with a sense of humour rarely seen among the Chinese. With such a firm control over her own life, she understood that by pleasing him she made her own life pleasurable too.

Julian was a man who trusted only his own judgement. If he thought she was the brightest and most vivacious woman in his life, then she would charm his mother too – if for no other reason than her dual ability to please him in bed and delight their guests in the dining room.

Julian was astonished at how many dresses she had. Lin told him that they had all been bought when she was much younger, before she moved to Wuhan. The servants looked after them now, keeping them scented with lavender. Julian took a step back and looked at her. The things she said never ceased to astonish him. It made her more desirable than ever, and her aura of mystery delighted him. In particular, he was glad that she had shaken off her dull university woman's garb. He had never found her more appealing than when she was dressed in the traditional clothes of a young Mandarin lady.

'Where do you get this kind of fabric?' he asked, touching the padded brocade of her coat. He was really thinking about the kind of woman's body that could be wrapped up in such extraordinary colours. She told him she would let him see for himself, led him out of the park at a quick pace and hailed a taxi, which took them downtown. When she found the shop she was looking for she whisked him inside and pointed to the rolls and bundles of cloth. With Lin's help he chose five bolts of silk, each with different colours and patterns, two of the same kind as her dress. She told him the manager would take care of everything, and he wrote out his mother's address in England.

Before he knew it Lin had paid for everything, shipping included. He did not know what to say. He could see that Lin wanted to treat him. Seeing him nonplussed, she said: 'Europeans don't fight over the bills, am I right? Well it's a long-standing Chinese habit to fight to pay. You can pay next time if you wish, and buy me whatever you like.'

The shop manager appeared again. With much bowing and scraping he said in broken English that he wanted to give Julian two gifts to thank him for doing business with him. He clapped his hands and immediately one of his assistants carried over two delicately wrought glass fish, each with an orange stripe along its flank. These too, he promised, would also arrive safely in England.

Lin smiled then ushered Julian out into the street again. He suddenly felt depressed at his stupid Western man's pride. He looked down the street, disconsolate. Once again Lin sensed what he was thinking. 'Don't be upset,' she said, squeezing his arm. 'Your mother will never know.' But that was wrong. His mother must know everything; he could not leave something like that out of his letters to her.

They walked together down the crowded street, taking pleasure in the mild winter's day and the garishly decorated shop windows. The padded blouses of the young shopgirls made them look shapeless, but their long almond-shaped eyes were lovely. The flower girl was selling several kinds of flowers, and it seemed that spring was in the air.

★

The theatre was packed but somehow Lin got hold of two front-row tickets. They had to sit this close, she said, because the leading man was 'the most handsome in the world'. Not only that, but a wonderful singer, too, and a brilliant actor. Women only had to touch him with their fingertips and they fainted; just watching him made them wet with excitement.

Lin had told Julian this in bed, before they left for the theatre. She could never have brought herself to say such things anywhere else. The very idea made them laugh.

Julian looked round curiously, to see who these women with such a vivid sexual imagination might be, and how they prepared for their great night out. Most were very glamorously dressed. Fortunately, Lin said, modern intellectuals did not go to the traditional theatre, let alone plays of this kind, which were regarded as obscene by educated audiences. There would be no risk of their running into acquaintances.

'Well, then we will be free to respond!' Julian whispered in Lin's ear. But it was so noisy, with everybody laughing and talking loudly, that his whisper was inaudible.

He waited for the curtain to rise, but there wasn't one, only a backdrop of deep crimson flannel. On the stage were a table, a chair and a long black box, which Lin told him was meant to represent a coffin. Then the opera began, with a loud clanging of gongs and drums, but the lights over the theatre seats were not dimmed, nor did the noise abate until an actor appeared on stage

A woman appeared making a high-pitched wail; she was beautiful but very heavily made up, dressed entirely in white. Lin explained the story to him. This character was mourning her husband — not so much singing, Julian thought, as emitting a long, sharp, whining cry. Her husband was the Daoist master Zhuang Zi, who had been away from home for many years, studying various people and places in order to try and establish a theory of universal law. She had waited patiently but her only reward had been to see him brought back to her in a coffin.

When she had finished her wailing a young man strode onto the stage with another crash from the gongs; he was also very beautiful, striking a highly artificial pose, singing a single line of music. Tremendous applause followed and the man sitting next to Julian let out a deafening, prolonged shout of approval: '*Hao...!*' while others all around him did the same. It seemed nothing would make them stop, but when the theatre eventually quietened down again the actor produced a fan from his sleeve and paced round the stage with quick steps, sweeping the audience with his gaze. In a shrill voice, drawing out his syllables in the most mannered way imaginable, he said that he was Zhuang Zi's devoted follower, the Prince of Chu. He was here under orders from the King to invite Zhuang Zi to become the new Prime Minister of the country. But he could see that he was too late. The only thing he could do was bow to the great man's coffin, and to Zhuang's widow, and offer his sympathy.

Julian did not know what to make of it. The stage was almost completely bare, simpler than even the most avant-garde stage design he had seen in London and Paris. But the actors' voices were really hideous – high-pitched and painful to listen to – and when they were not singing they were moving around in a preposterous dance.

But he could see that the man acting the Prince of Chu was in a class of his own. His dancing was extremely nimble – neat, short steps and long, loose swoops as he held Zhuang's wife by the hand. After a few minutes of this his manner changed and he began eyeing her more closely, letting his gaze jerk up and down her body in little leaps, while the percussion kept up its sibilant rattle. Then he gestured as if touching her, starting with her embroidered shoes and gradually working up over her legs and thighs. Eventually both he and Zhuang's wife turned to face the audience and made darting sideways movements with their eyes, leering at each other. It made them look ridiculous, Julian thought, like a couple of courting ducks, but they obviously did not feel foolish themselves, fluttering their long sleeves and flickering their fans. When they had finished there was more wild clapping, mixed with a good deal of giggling.

Evidently, with the Prince's attentions, all Zhuang's wife's sadness had evaporated. In fact, they now seemed desperately in love, swearing their devotion to each other as they danced, singing that they 'wanted to be birds flying wing to wing, to be two lotus petals touching'.

Suddenly the Prince lurched backwards, flinging up his hands and complaining that he had a terrible headache. No sooner had he said this than he did an enormous backward somersault, while a gong crashed explosively. Zhuang's wife circled round him like a wounded bird, waving her arms and singing on a high, keening note. The Prince lifted his head then hurled himself over again in a series of smaller somersaults. Julian supposed he was trying to tell her that he was dying.

When the Prince eventually pulled himself upright again, someone appeared on stage dressed in nondescript black clothes. He gave the Prince a cup of tea.

'I thought there were only two people in the whole thing,' Julian whispered to Lin.

'There are,' she said. 'This one isn't part of the play.'

Julian blinked in disbelief and settled himself again as the stagehand disappeared, taking the chair and the teacup with him. The Prince promptly launched himself into a new aria. According to Lin he was saying that his fever, the illness that drove him to these extraordinary leaps and convulsions, could only be cured by eating the brain of a human being. 'But where would you get such a thing?' Zhuang's wife asked him. The Prince of Chu raised a trembling hand and pointed at the coffin. She understood immediately, and gave a cry of such extraordinary length that only a second wave of cheering and barracking from the audience brought it to a close.

'What's going on now?' Julian asked. 'Why is the audience so happy about her misery?'

'They are cheering the fake play,' Lin said, 'not the real play.'

'What do you mean? I don't understand.'

Lin gave her sideways smile. 'You Westerners are too foolish to appreciate Chinese opera,' she said.

When Julian looked back to the stage he saw that Zhuang's wife had taken off her white mourning dress and was now wearing a tight red dancing blouse, in which she was circling the coffin menacingly, wielding an axe. When she brushed against it she stopped and lifted the blade.

But the coffin opened before she struck down, and out jumped Zhuang Zi – played by the same actor who had been the Prince; he had not even changed his costume. Once again Zhuang's wife recoiled in horror, realizing that all through his courtship 'the Prince' had in fact been her husband, testing her faithfulness. Zhuang Zi immediately began a long solo during which his wife did nothing but sob behind first one sleeve and then the other. As he ended, she began wielding the axe again, apparently determined to do away with herself. Zhuang Zi seemed in no hurry to stop her, but stood silent and complacent while she sang an aria of her own, which she finished by making a single slicing gesture across her throat and collapsing onto the stage.

Zhuang Zi responded with a deep bow, while his wife rose gracefully from the ground and followed suit, at the same time throwing a sideways leer at her 'husband'. Lin and Julian rose from their seats amid the cheering and followed the red carpet that led to the foyer.

'This is really incomprehensible,' said Julian, not caring how grouchy he sounded. 'Why is the audience so chaotic?'

'Chinese theatre's like that,' Lin replied. 'Everyone knows the play by heart, and they only stop making a racket when the best moments come.'

'No, I mean how could their moral standards be so chaotic? They applaud the widow when she flirts, but they approve of her suicide, too.'

'Well,' came the answer, 'if we were all completely moral then what would be the point of plays? If all we ever did was flirt, how would we have social order?'

Lin stopped abruptly, realizing she was upsetting them both. She took off her glasses and folded them into their case; there were more operas scheduled to follow this one, but they had had enough.

They pushed their way through the foyer and out into the street. As they stood in the darkness, Lin said that she had a headache and wanted to go home. Julian nodded then hailed a taxi and sat beside her, wondering what to make of everything he had seen. It was certainly very exotic and spectacular, but if he tried to make sense of it he would soon have a splitting headache himself

He said good night to Lin when they reached her father's house, and drove on to the hotel. He realized with some slight embarrassment that he was exhausted, and could do with a night alone.

But Lin did not come the next day. Their usual time to meet was ten in the morning at the latest. He waited until noon, then went to the restaurant downstairs and had lunch by himself. He did not want to hang around the hotel any longer, and remembered that friends in London had suggested he go and see Sir Harold Acton, who was teaching at Peking University. So, armed with Acton's address, he set forth.

Acton lived in a courtyard house off a small alley. The numerous rooms looked out onto the courtyard, with its trees and benches, and were light and comfortably furnished. Acton greeted Julian with, 'How like Roger Fry you look! I thought you were him for a moment.' Julian had been about to apologize for turning up without an appointment, but saw that Acton was as relaxed as any of the Bloomsbury crowd and no apology was necessary.

There was a tall, good-looking young Chinese man in the drawing room, whom Acton introduced as his student, Chen.

He said something to Chen in Chinese and from their eyes Julian at once understood their relationship. Acton was embarrassed but Julian simply smiled pleasantly. He was used to homosexuals and bore no prejudices. Mother's boyfriend, Duncan Grant, often brought male lovers home, sometimes young sailors who would sneak a painting away with them the next morning on their way out. Fortunately they never knew which were the valuable ones. Even the children of the house knew what was going on, and when they saw some new lover arrive would laugh and shout, 'Here comes another burglar!'

Realizing that Julian was teaching in Wuhan, Acton and Chen immediately brought up the subject of Professor Cheng and Lin the novelist. Had they come back to Peking? If so, maybe the New Moon Society members still living in the city should get together. There was a group of new poets making their names, many of whom attended Acton's English literature class at Peking University.

The ubiquitous New Moon Society! Julian decided not to say that Lin was in Peking: Acton and Chen seemed to know too much for him to feel comfortable. He was preparing to make his excuses and leave when Acton stopped him. 'Surely you're not off before you've had a drink?'

'A drink?'

'Of course. You're alone in Peking. And as the Chinese saying goes, "The wine should flow freely when real friends meet."'

Chen went to the kitchen to make arrangements for dinner. Acton said that he already felt Chinese; in fact, he was sure his eyes were growing more slanted by the day! In Peking one met a lot of European intellectuals – the gifted young Cambridge critic William Empson for one. It was rather a contrast to provincial Chinese cities, where foreigners were either businessmen or missionaries. Acton and some friends had just come back from a trip to Chengde Hill Palace, an ideal place for winter hunting. No one who really appreciated Chinese life could be homesick for Europe.

Julian, however, sensed that Acton, for all his protestations, was still a lonely man, just as he himself had felt today when he was waiting in the hotel.

Acton took him to another room to show off his collection of antiques. As they crossed the courtyard he told Julian, 'Peking is the last paradise on earth. You may think that I am only saying this to justify my self-imposed exile here. But think of European society. There is no escaping its moralistic judgements and social conservatism, apart from among the few free spirits of your Bloomsbury set.' He heaved a long sigh. 'The damned Japanese army has been getting nearer. Just this December the Communist students staged a well-organized demonstration, supposedly in protest at Japanese encroachment but actually trying to force the Government to stop hunting the Red Army. We heard about a similar demonstration in Wuhan. Did you see it?'

Julian fingered the slight scar on his forehead but kept silent. 'The Japanese...the Communists...' Acton shook his head despairingly. 'How long can we expect paradise to last?'

Early next morning, while Julian was still in bed at the hotel, Lin came. Too many drinks with Acton had given him a hangover and a bad headache. Lin, however, made light of his discomfort. She said she knew a place that would cure any headache; in fact, she had already called a taxi to take them to the Western Hills on the outskirts of Peking, so he had better dress quickly.

Julian wondered whether he could ever understand China, let alone Chinese women. Lin did not get involved in apologies or explanations for failing to show up the day before. She had simply thought of the best way to make it up to him.

Anyway, after a day without her Julian was in no mood to argue. Surrounded by magnificent scenery and pretty women, and enjoying Lin's skill in the Art of Love with its promises of longevity and immortality, he really had nothing to complain about. He found it all immensely stimulating, even down to the gaudily decorated shops, the shrill funeral music and odd public scenes, like the extravagant tears of the owner of a dog that had frozen to death during the night.

Lin took them to the Western Hills Hot-Spring Inn. Their room was dominated by a huge hot-spring bath tub: as he took Lin in his arms and lifted her into it, he thought that he, like Acton, did not miss England one little bit.

He had only been without Lin for a day, but now he craved her with a desperate physical need. His body seemed beyond his control, as if it belonged to someone else.

The marble tub was filled with hot, vaporous water up to the waist. One side sloped gently. As they lay back he was filled with desire. Devouring her body with his eyes he had the odd sensation that he was the Emperor and she the jewel of his royal harem. Naked, her smooth shape half submerged in water, she was far lovelier than in any elaborate dress. Her pubic mound looked like a piece of clear jade underwater. He lifted her buttocks with his hand so that it was completely exposed. Compulsively he caressed her. Her skin felt like silk under his hand. He could never have enough of her. 'There's no woman like you in the West.'

The hair on his chest and belly floated in the water. It looked a little like seaweed, in crude contrast with Lin's hairless body. She stroked the hair. 'There's no man like you in China, either.'

His headache had long disappeared. She held him in her arms and whispered, 'Slowly. Slowly. We have a whole day ahead of us.'

She began to talk to him. 'In the *Jade Chamber Classic*, women like me are described like this: "Their pubic mound is high, no hair adorns it, but they have abundant lubrication; they are aged over twenty-five and are childless." See how exactly I fit the definition? Even my age. It is also stated in the book: "Those men who have not yet learned the Art will not be harmed by these women." So, you don't have to be afraid.'

'Why should I be afraid of you?' said Julian, slipping his hand between her legs again.

'And don't be surprised, either.' But Julian was not listening. He went under the water and kissed her nipples, then lifted his head and, shaking the drops out of his hair, said, 'I'm no man. I'm just a big, cuddly wolf.' And pushing open her legs he pressed himself impatiently into her.

Lin had told Julian that bathing was an important part of Daoist culture, and lovemaking in the bath was regarded as an art; one Lin had never had a chance to try until today. Now she could feel that when he withdrew there was a pressure caused by the water vacuum, and when he pushed forward the hot water was squeezed far up inside her, as if it was reaching right up to her heart.

Her face was above the water and he could see her orgasm approach. Her skin was intensely flushed, her eyes were glazed and her hands moved down from his neck to his legs, pressing him hard against her. Her voice sank to a kind of cooing, then turned again into her almost mesmeric, rhythmic moans, as if in her ecstasy she had reached an altered level of consciousness.

Julian had never known such happiness. The Romans knew how to make the bath the focus of erotic enjoyment, with the massage, the bathhouse women, the pornographic murals. He had never expected to find himself in a sort of Chinese Pompeii, had never imagined the intensity of pleasure that sex in hot water brought to women.

He was no longer a liberal intellectual born of Bloomsbury, nor Professor Bell, nor even an Englishman, but pure yang in union with yin. Inside her her muscles wrestled him with the help of hot water, and her slippery breasts, belly and legs slid up and down his until he shook in excitement. He felt that he was being carried along on a tide, higher and higher. On the crest of the waves his orgasm was long and violent. And then he saw, marvelling a little, how his semen, like tiny jellyfish, swam from inside her and rose in the clear water.

Under the dimmed lamp, Lin was in Japanese-style pyjamas of a soft yellow colour. The jacket hung loose off her shoulders and showed parts of her body as she moved. Now she was standing in front of Julian, who reclined on the high pillows of the tatami bed looking appreciatively at her. They would stay here for the night.

They had no idea how much time had passed. The moon was high and bright in the sky. The curtains were open and it shed a cold, blue light into the room. This quiet time of night was the best time to practise qigong, said Lin. Her mother had often woken her at midnight to do so, so that her body should receive both celestial and earthly energy, from moonlight and dew. They had often practised it beside the lotus pond in the garden.

'Why do you sing when you make love?' Julian asked. 'It's different every time.'

It was not singing, Lin explained. The ululation was produced naturally by the breath drifting through the throat while the mind was in deep meditation. It was the result of breathing exercises, but by itself could also help to control the breathing. It was like the undulation of trees in a forest, or the wind blowing over the grasslands: it was musical only in that sense. She did not do it intentionally; that was why the tune, if any, was never repeated.

She took a few steps back from him, then sat down with legs crossed in the lotus position. Her posture was straight. Her hands were placed in front of her, with the fingers forming the shape of a flower. Her whole body looked like a glimmering golden lotus.

He rose and approached, but Lin stopped him with her eyes, telling him to sit and watch.

Water should be boiled with bamboo leaves and peach kernels and allowed to cool to a suitable temperature. Then you should undress and plunge in and expel the used air from the body. But her mother had preferred the 'dry technique'. Lin demonstrated. Initially it looked like self-massage, but far more sophisticated. Her fingers started in between the eyebrows and the eye corners, progressed along her nose and circled her whole face nine times. Then her fingers combed her hair and began to trace the length of her whole body. She held her breasts in her palms while twisting her nipples deftly with her fingertips. Finally she reached her vulva and showed him an even more intricate display of fingerwork.

It looked to him like a woman's masturbation, in the same way as her 'ululation' was a variation on other women's sex cries during lovemaking. Yet it was more than that. Ritualizing their sexual self-expression meant that intellectual Chinese women like Lin need not feel ashamed.

During her self-massage her pyjamas gaped wider and finally fell from her altogether. She was in a kind of trance, her body still present but her mind in an altered state. Waves of pleasure crossed her face. He now knew that before meeting him Lin had always satisfied her sexual urges like this. Perhaps that was what maintained her youthfulness.

He felt sorry for her. She did not have anyone in her life to give her the gratification she needed. And he was suddenly overcome by fear, and felt excluded by her 'self-cultivation'. The two contradictory feelings seized him at the same moment, so strongly that he moved forward impulsively to take her in his arms.

The tenderness he felt surprised him. He had always been suspicious of any affection beyond sex. He loved sex for the sake of sex, sex for pleasure. Any emotional attachment was likely to bring the torment of responsibility.

But this woman in his arms had spent so many years of her

lonely life in these freakish exercises: her sole consolation came from this Daoist cult. Her years of girlhood and her married life must have been marred by physical and spiritual solitude – thirty-five years, and she would be thirty-six this year. Julian knew better than most people what loneliness was, and what kind of individuals suffered from it.

It took him back to his earliest memories, when he was scarcely more than a baby. He heard the adults talking in the next room, the clamour of their voices mingling with laughter. And he was left alone in his cot. On those evenings he rebelled by crying as loudly and insistently as he could. Sometimes his mother heard him, and would stop all discussion, no matter what the topic, to make sure that he was really all right. Aunt Virginia often complained that after his birth a little devil came to interrupt every Bloomsbury gathering.

His continuing sense of isolation – he had never lost it – explained, in part, why he had come to the Far East, and why he felt drawn to this Chinese woman. His loneliness, her loneliness – they were both scared of loneliness and craved each other's care. He still remembered the acute despair that enveloped him as a child, when he cried to no avail, failed to attract attention even from his mother and was left to gaze blankly at the ceiling, at the shadows thrown by the furniture in the room and at the grey sky outside the window.

Chapter Eight

February 1936. Snow had fallen heavily all night; now it reflected brightly on buildings and passers-by. Lin and Julian, in a horse-drawn carriage, drove through streets neatly lined with tall poplars; Julian in a black coat and hat, Lin in a dark-red cloak and lighter skirt. Her hair was tucked into a hat and the frosty air gave her cheeks a youthful glow.

Julian had been writing a poem throughout the previous evening and early that morning. He had left the desk littered with crumpled paper. The winter vacation was drawing to an end and it was time to go back to Wuhan. Lin was about to arrange their return train tickets.

Julian was relieved. She was aware that they had to return to Wuhan, and had started making preparations. Had she not broached the matter herself, he would have been loath to mention it. It was easier to pretend that their days together would never end, that the responsibilities that awaited them in Wuhan no longer existed.

Her red outfit against the whiteness of the snow struck his eyes painfully.

On the street some children played with a top-heavy snowman, which began slowly to collapse as they passed by. Acton's emotional declaration that Peking was the last paradise on earth came to Julian's mind. The carriage turned the corner and entered a broad side street. They spotted a street performer with a performing monkey dressed in a bizarrely coloured jacket.

'You were born in the year of the Monkey,' Lin had teased him a few days before.

'I suppose that means I'm always up to no good, does it?'

'Well, you won't change the character you were born with,' she replied. Then, as if to herself, 'Born in the year of the Monkey...Eight years younger than I am!'

He wondered what she meant by that, and could not think of a reply. He had no idea what lay beneath her words. During their stay in Peking she had been so happy and relaxed, and so loving, with the exception of their one gloomy outing to the theatre. However, they had not talked about the future. This was beginning to bother him. Without knowing what her feelings were, he could not bring himself to start the discussion. Was she waiting for him to take the initiative? He had no way of knowing. One thing was clear: she was capable of complete silence. The more she wanted to talk about something, the more savagely she would repress it.

He realized that the Chinese cleared only their own courtyards and gateways of snow. Against the outer walls of the courtyards in the alleyways it piled up in drifts and buttresses, while at street level passers-by left deep, black footprints. The thaw was setting in. A hawker waded past them through the wet snow, selling sticks of candied wild fruit. Lin stopped their driver and bought two, handing one to Julian. He took a bite. The fruits were tangy and sweet. Lin smiled, saying she knew he would like them. Peking was the best place to get them.

The carriage sped away, taking Lin to her father's house and leaving him in the alley. Julian was trying to recall Acton's house number when he saw Sir Harold himself standing at the gate, wearing a pink woollen scarf.

The courtyard belonged to the famous old painter, Qi Baishi. 'His name means "White Stone",' Acton said. 'Strange name, isn't it? He's adored by the Germans. Definitely the number one Chinese painter this century.'

Julian knocked at the door. The servant opened but refused to let him in until he caught sight of Acton standing behind him.

When they had been drinking a few days ago, Acton had boasted of his art collection. Then he'd offered to introduce Julian to a neighbour, a painter – the Cézanne of the Orient, he said, the Chinese Matisse. Best of all, his prices were reasonable. 'You could buy some interesting things from him.'

Julian felt that he had already bought enough Chinese artefacts to fill a gallery. Yet he had not spent a lot on them. No wonder so many Westerners bought up vast quantities of porcelain, jade and antiques, both genuine and forged. But he was won over by Acton. His parents and their friends had made their reputations by mounting exhibitions of the Post-Impressionists in London. They had shocked and shaped the artistic taste of Britain, and made Bloomsbury a byword for modernism. Perhaps he could do likewise.

The servant ushered them along winding corridors until, after many twists and turns through a series of courtyards, they were in the celebrated artist's studio. It was neither as large nor as messy as the studio of a Western painter. Everything in it was neat and tidy. Qi Baishi was over seventy, but he looked strong, his face unwrinkled and his long beard still black. He wore a small skullcap and glasses. He was surrounded by a small group of men and women, who watched him respectfully. Some were assistants, others students.

The old man waited for Julian and Acton to speak. After a few stumbling words, Julian left the talking to Acton. The latter spoke Chinese fluently with a perfect Peking accent and almost unctuous politeness. He clearly charmed the old man. Paper was spread on the wide table and Julian was asked to choose between flowers, birds, fish, insects, crabs, lobsters, chickens, ducks, monkeys, snakes…

Julian, who found it hard to take this seriously, settled on two crabs. The assistants fixed the paper with paperweights and started grinding up the ink cake with two ink stones. The old man rolled up his sleeves, and, as if by magic, two crabs appeared before their eyes within a couple of minutes. One was a little darker than the other. Their sixteen legs and four pairs of pincers waved in the air.

Acton asked, 'And what is this splendid couple up to?' The old man burst out laughing. Without answering, he picked up a tiny brush and dabbed a little deep black ink, in four fine dots. Now the two crabs were making eyes at each other. Julian's own eyes opened wide and Acton applauded. So this was the art of the Chinese Matisse, who painted as fast as a printing press. Western painters would have slaved for weeks to produce two such crabs.

'Can I buy it?' Julian asked. 'Yes,' came the reply. 'I charge six US dollars per square foot.' This was a discount price for a friend of Acton, who, it seemed, had often brought Westerners here. The manner in which the old man fixed a price was as unusual as his style of painting. He hesitated. This was not a Matisse, for sure, only a playful sketch. He found it hard to believe that genuine art could really be produced just like that and sold by the square foot. Evidently both China's art and its market were beyond the understanding of Europeans. 'Can I pay by cheque?' said Julian, still a little nonplussed. Certainly. 'Mr Ai-ke-dun' was an old friend.

There was no pen in the studio, so Julian had to use the painting brush to write his cheque, which he managed with a certain awkwardness. The old man gave Acton two miniature paintings as gifts, adding his signature. As they were about to leave, Acton covertly indicated to Julian a woman in a Western blouse wearing thick red lipstick.

The old man saw them to the door of the room, and Acton assiduously complimented his host in the traditional Chinese style. Once outside, he told Julian that the woman was the old man's current concubine, a gift from a friend. She had given him six children in the last seven years – clearly the old man was productive in more ways than one.

Julian was mildly shocked, and the scroll in his hand felt

suddenly as if the crabs had come alive. Acton's Chinese Matisse could go on living for another thirty years and father a large number of children. Perhaps the lightning creativity that gave birth to these two crabs was actually a by-product of his sexual prowess.

Acton warned him to be on the alert against burglary now that he owned a painting by the great master.

Lin came the next day, and smiled when she saw the painting Julian had bought. It was a treasure to bequeath to his children, she said. But then she stopped herself...the conversation was straying too near the forbidden topic.

When the sun rose high the snow melted rapidly, leaving pockets only between the tiles or in the forks of branches. Lin had an indigo satin dress on, with an orchid pattern in silver. Though Julian had noticed that her earlobes were pierced, this was the first time he had seen her wearing earrings. Each had two sapphires, the lower one bigger than the upper, set in silver, and they went well with her dress.

She took Julian to a restaurant called the Dong Lai Shun, which was well known for its hotpot-style lamb cooked at the table. The pot, heated by charcoal, contained the soup. One used chopsticks to dip paper-thin lamb slices into it. The lamb cooked instantly and was then fished out and eaten. It was delicious, but since the slices were so thin it was not a meal to be eaten in a hurry. The sauce, minced scallion and pak choi were served as an accompaniment.

They sat in privacy behind screens, and Julian noticed a number of carved water birds on the back of their chairs, with long feathers on their backs and at their throats, beard-like. Lin told him that these were called 'love ducks' in Chinese, because they habitually nestled close to each other.

Their conversation moved to literature. She felt the subject matter of her fiction was too limited, judged by the current standards of the 'revolutionary thirties'. Yet how could she avoid basing her writing on the society within which she moved: wealthy families made up of patriarchs with numerous concubines and feckless children?

'Like me?' Julian said jokingly. Then he took his poem out of his pocket. As Lin took it to read, Julian added, 'Not out loud!'

Post Coitum
Across, between, th'entangling net,
  Fragile Venus, bothered Mars.
The meshes of the trap are set,
  Red-rusted as the tidal stars,
Penetration Nature yet
  Admits; integument debars:
Sepia crustacea *can beget*
  As well amid their clicketing wars.
Crab-limbed lock in ocean hold
  Of saline mucus foundering deep;

'Post Coitum!' Lin covered her mouth to stop herself from giggling like a girl. 'Very explicit. But what is '*sepia crustacea*'? Lin had difficulty in following the tightly knit lines with their many Latin derivatives.

'It's just another way of describing an inky sea creature.'

'So you've borrowed from Qi Baishi's menagerie: lobster, squid, crab and so on.'

She was right, that was in fact how the poem came into its present shape. But she did not show the admiration he had expected.

'Don't you like it?'

'Of course I like it. I'm an ink fish, moved to and fro by the water. I'm the deep ocean itself, gathering the saline mucus. I'm a crab that flounders deep in your meshes. It's about me. I love it.'

'But what about the poem itself? What if it had nothing to do with you?'

'It's very sensual,' Lin said. 'But you have already shown the poem to another woman, haven't you? You wrote it for her.' Julian was dumbfounded. 'How could I have? You know it was only finished yesterday evening when you were out of the hotel?'

'Exactly. It was finished when you were writing to your mother.'

Julian was lost for words. She was acutely sensitive. She had fathomed his dependence on his mother, to whom he was actually more like a Platonic lover than a son.

At that moment the waitress brought a number of strange dishes: black mushrooms, pine mushrooms, amaranth, taro, bamboo shoots, sliced sea cucumber.

After she had gone, Lin said with great sincerity, 'I just wish that I could fall in love with your mother, too, to share your intimacy.'

Those words struck deep into his heart. Julian was overwhelmed. He had never met a woman whose intuition had led her to see so clearly the multiple layers of this relationship. He felt confused about it himself. Yet she, with her limited command of English, had struck home.

On impulse Julian took out another piece of paper. 'These are the last four lines of the poem I showed you. Now who do you think it was written for?'

Escape, sea gale winged through the cold
  Red sunsets, black bent trees, the steep
English bird-voiced cliffs; till old,
  Tangled across the bars, we sleep.

Lin looked at it for a long time. Suddenly she was weeping uncontrollably, soundlessly, surrendering absolutely to her tears.

Julian's heart tightened. He took her in his arms. Still unsure of his own feelings and whether he should put them into words, he had not intended to show Lin the last four lines, but his resolve had crumbled in the face of her intensity.

She pushed him away a little, took out a handkerchief to wipe her face and said, 'It's nothing. I know this is only a poem. But those words – "Till old…we sleep" – I want to give you a gift, to say thank you. I want to take you somewhere you won't ever forget, not till you die.'

As the black door closed behind them, the noise of the streets was shut out. The sun was starting to go down in the west. In the days that followed, when Julian tried to recall what had happened, he retained only jumbled memories mixed with a feeling of great longing.

The outer courtyard did not herald anything remarkable. However, he would never forget what he experienced after they went through the second gate. He would, as Lin had said, remember it till he died.

The courtyard held the customary rock garden and a pool, behind which was a tall, lush green grove of bamboo. On the ornamental plum trees the blossom was withering, and fallen petals littered the water and the path.

The proprietress was an amiable middle-aged woman, neatly dressed, pleasant-looking. Lin talked to her in a Chinese so rapid that Julian was unable to make out a single word. The woman smiled courteously and led them down the narrow corridor on both sides of which were rows of rooms with sliding latticework doors. Above some doors there were lanterns. Other rooms seemed to hold people, but it was very quiet and the air was heavy with a peculiar smell, which Julian was unable to identify.

Lin turned to tell him that she had used her father's name so as to be sure to get the 'full treatment'. Only later did he come to know what that phrase meant.

They were led into a spacious but sparsely furnished room. The woman issued some orders in a low voice and took her leave. Then two maids came in to take their coats. The room was dimly lit by candles. Three heaters were burning pine charcoal. The bed, a northern Chinese brick bed with a wood-burning stove inside, was extraordinarily large, taking up most of the room. It was impeccably clean, with a carved mahogany headboard, a number of pillows and cushions, and bed covers of white fox fur. Over it hung a fine muslin curtain. The temperature was perfect, neither too hot nor too cold.

The two maids spread white embroidered covers on the bed and helped the guests off with their shoes. Another two maids brought in items that he did not recognize. Lin rearranged her hair, took some pillows and made herself comfortable on the bed. Propping her head on her hand, she smiled at Julian, who, with the air of a clumsy puppet, was having his outer garments removed by the maids. 'Relax,' she told him. 'Pay no attention to them.'

Within a few minutes the maids had put everything in place, retired noiselessly and closed the door. Only one remained in the room. She went to the door and bolted it.

Looking at the long pipe that the maid now placed in his hand, Julian realized this was an opium house. He remembered scenes from a Western documentary he had seen on China, showing squalid dens where people were hopelessly destroyed by their addiction. He certainly would not believe those so-called China watchers again. Between he and Lin there was a whole set of smoking paraphernalia, and the maid in her red silk blouse was kneeling, busy with all sorts of preparations. She picked some sort of paste from a small round box and held it on a wire rack above a small charcoal burner. The black paste melted, turned a brownish colour and started to form a golden bubble.

The maid picked up the bubble deftly with a long needle,

placed it in the bowl of the pipe and handed it to Julian.

Not knowing what to do with it, he deferred to Lin. She smiled and took the pipe from him, although she was clearly not an experienced smoker either. However, she managed to inhale, with two slight coughs, and he watched with fascination as the bubble grew smaller and finally disappeared with a slight pop. Julian gave a low murmur of admiration and Lin smiled apologetically. She had tried it only once before, when she had seen her mother smoking opium, but had forgotten how it should be done.

The second bubble was ready and Julian followed suit, inhaling slowly. He did better than Lin. His lungs filled with something which burned slightly but was fragrant and pleasantly stimulating.

He watched Lin opposite him on the bed. It was so warm in the room that both of them had stripped to their underwear. They smiled at each other as if in anticipation. How beautiful she looked. The surprising thing was that, although the maid was still with them, she now took off her last layer of clothing. Her long black hair hung down over her shoulders and, fixing her eyes on his, she stretched out sensuously, every part of her naked body revealed to him.

He could not manage four pipes. By the second pipe he was already floating heavenward, accompanied by a choir of angels. By the third he felt that he, too, could fly, unhindered by clothes. And then his clothes were gone, he was completely naked and unfettered, capable of anything. But where was she? Lin's place on the bed was empty and he felt her body on his. How good, he murmured.

The choir was still singing in his head. He felt as if every cell in his body was being transformed into something insubstantial, as she and he floated weightless together. Even Lin's body, nestled against his, seemed somehow incorporeal.

All of a sudden she was no longer there. Her lips had closed around his cock. A shock ran through his groin and he sprang erect. The feeling was almost too intense to bear. He uttered a groan. What was she was doing?

As a young boy at school he had read the English translation of the sixteenth-century Chinese novel, *The Golden Lotus*. He had little interest in its innumerable characters going about their mundane business. What impressed him most vividly were the women in the book who loved 'playing the flute' with their lovers. His Latin class was reading Julius Caesar, whose boastful *Gallic Wars* he found interminably boring, and which most students read secretly in tandem with an English translation. But there was Latin of different kind in *The Golden Lotus*, and it fired his imagination. He could still recite the passages where the flute was being played:

> *Caput mentulae lingua sua titillabat, et inter labra sursum deorsum volvebat... Mentulam in genas mollivit et in os recepit. Foramen titillabat et lingua nervum provocabat. Labris firme continuit et molliter movit...et continuo in os mulieris exiit semen quod tarde sorbuit.*

His Latin improved by leaps and bounds, to the astonishment of his teacher, and the flute-playing women accompanied his masturbation. But none of his girlfriends in England had been willing to try it out. Some found it too sordid even to listen to, and accused him of perversion. He had never dared to bring it up with Lin, fearing that, unlike the female protagonists of *The Golden Lotus*, she was too well bred for that kind of thing.

Now Lin had thrown off her last inhibitions. So any woman – even any Chinese woman, ancient or modern – could enjoy doing it.

And she was using her breasts, pressed against his balls, and her hands as well as her mouth. She lifted her head slightly and her tongue licked the ridge round his glans, the most sensitive of all places.

He was in a sort of paradise where a heavenly choir sang in seraphic harmony. Lin was an Imperial concubine, naked, flute in hand, and her body glowed the colours of the rainbow. She was his favourite, the sublime flautist whose technique was famed around the capital.

He had to hold her. He pulled her up into his arms. She lifted her head and when she looked at him with that face aroused and beautiful, his breathing, which had relaxed a little, quickened again.

Lin made a sign and the maid, who had long since cleared the smoking set from the bed, took off her simple clothes. She was young, about seventeen, and her body was lean with small, tight breasts. Without being asked, she lay face down between them. Lin lay on top of her with her buttocks at the maid's waist, so that the lower half of her body was propped high in the air.

Julian had seen such a scene, in which the maid was used as a cushion as well as a sexual stimulant, in an erotic painting, but he had dismissed it as just another Chinese fantasy. Now it proved otherwise. Lin was offering her most secret parts to him. Her vulva seemed to shine white in the gloom, her labia were swollen and glistening, her clitoris like a little cherry. Her whole body opened up to him. He could no longer contain himself.

She was still wriggling into position when he pulled himself on top of her. She gripped him and he was inside her at once and so deeply that she cried out in wild excitement. Then the maid heaved and lowered her body, catching both of them up in an undulating motion so their three bodies swayed in a kind of rhythmic dance.

The flames in the stove licked higher, the muslin curtain flapped crazily, they were carried upwards by the heat of the forest fire. Higher, then higher they rose.

Totally controlled by the two women, Julian's cock was forcibly pushed in and out. Drunk with pleasure, he had a strange conviction that all the sensual pleasures that life could possibly hold for him would be exhausted in this intoxicating climax.

How much time had passed? It seemed to be flashing by, yet also to be holding him in a slow embrace. Another pipe was placed in his lips. Succoured by the miraculous bubble, he drifted into a half sleep. Somehow, he had switched positions with Lin. Now his head was pillowed on the maid's soft hips and between Lin's legs, which also rested across the young servant's body. Then he noticed the long mirror set into the headboard, in which he saw reflected a Chinese painting of flowers and birds.

His organ was inside Lin's mouth, wrung by her tongue, rolling in saliva, fuelling the flickering sparks that shot out from his glans. He almost cried out, feeling that his body was being set aflame in her throat. A power was nearly tearing him apart. Lin's arms, as if in despair, were flung in the air, and her whole pelvis was violently twitching. He called out her name. As if shaken by thunder, his body, their bodies together, were juddering into pieces.

The next day Julian sat alone on the train southbound to Wuhan. In his hand was a yellow silk handkerchief. This morning, after going to the hotel to fetch his luggage, the two of them had taken a taxi to the railway station. In the taxi Lin gave him the handkerchief. Stitched on one corner in yellow silk thread he found the letter K. The silk had a pattern of bamboo leaves woven into it, just like her dress. He had once heard that yellow had long been esteemed in China as the colour of the Imperial throne, but in modern China yellow was considered the colour of eroticism. Now he was at a loss to know what she meant by it. She said only, carry it as long as you wish.

Why did she embroider a K on it? To acknowledge her position? To tell him she was no longer jealous of those other women before her? Or just to show that she was now sure she could surpass all the other women in his life?

He could not sleep. The train wheels beat a monotonous rhythm on the rails and the carriages rocked and swayed gently. They were travelling through the country he had last seen over a month ago. He could not stop thinking about Lin. She had found her way inside him and sown a seed that was germinating frighteningly fast.

In the opium house he had fallen asleep in that awesome bed immediately after the last savage orgasm. He woke up once and saw Lin lying naked and asleep, too, unlike the other times, when she had stayed awake after lovemaking. Her head was still between his legs, her black hair dishevelled and spread across his thigh while both arms embraced his other leg and her face nestled against his groin, her lips still gently pressed against it.

Julian had never seen any woman surrender to sexual desire like that. The opium, he supposed, brought one's most deeply hidden desires to the surface. Looking at her tranquil face and sensual body he could no longer hold out against his feelings. He lightly removed her hands and lowered himself into her arms. He had never before cared about any woman so much. He felt certain that he could never love any woman more than this. Yes, he loved Lin, he was now very sure of it. He lay down alongside her, holding her, caressing her gently and cradling her head as if she were a child. He felt that his heart was full of love, and fell tranquilly asleep again.

He recalled all that this morning when the taxi arrived at the crowded railway station. Lin said goodbye without leaving the taxi, so as to avoid bumping into anyone she knew. After a pause she told him she had begun to like Wuhan because that was where she had met him.

Julian was about to say something when a siren started to wail sharply. They had no idea what it meant, and the taxi hurriedly accelerated away taking Lin with it.

He turned this remark of hers over and over now on the train. At the time he had wanted to respond, 'No, I do not like Wuhan, because I want to stay here with you.' The pain in his heart stopped him. More than anything, he now wanted to spend the rest of his life with this woman. Precisely because of this, he needed to think hard before he spoke. His love weighed upon him. He had to be utterly responsible for everything he said, to weigh everything against his innermost feelings.

As the train headed south he began to sink into desperation, the desperation of being driven into her arms, of losing his freedom to choose. What would love be like once the affair turned into something more permanent? Lin had told him that he would never forget his experience in Peking – 'till you die', those were her words. Yet she had avoided all talk of their future, only weeping desperately when reading his poem. Why?

Perhaps she knew that it was futile to talk. Unless he accepted a commitment to their love no promises he made would stand the test of time.

When the train arrived in Zhengzhou it was already noon the next day. He saw almost all the passengers swarm out onto the platform and scramble to buy a newspaper. A Frenchman sharing his carriage acquired one and sat reading it, shaking his head. Julian couldn't understand even the headlines, so he asked what was the matter.

'War! War!' the man said.

Julian told him to explain in French, and learned that the recent clash between the Japanese and Chinese armies at the Great Wall north of Peking had led to Japanese warplanes overflying Peking in a blatant threat. The Chinese

145

Government had issued a very serious protest.

Right at the time when he was leaving Peking! So the wailing siren when he ran for his train was an air-raid warning. It felt as if the Japanese fascists were sending him a reminder.

'This kind of thing has happened several times before,' his companion went on. 'The Chinese Government doesn't want an all-out war with Japan at the moment. They will yield their land inch by inch, and fight only at the negotiating table.' He rolled his eyes. '*Mais Pékin est fini! Pékin est fini!*'

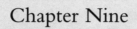

Chapter Nine

It was seven days since Julian's return. The new term had started, but because he was ill he had not resumed his classes

In the kitchen Vole told him that Professor Cheng had been to Hankou railway station to meet his wife, who had just returned from Peking. She had come back laden with luggage, all gifts from friends and relatives.

Julian was noncommittal. He had come down for some milk. All milk and water in China had to be boiled before drinking, so every morning Vole boiled quantities of fresh milk and set it aside to cool. Julian loved cold milk, and would gulp down glassfuls at a time.

'Mrs Dean looked wonderful, at least ten years younger!' said Vole. 'She must have been burning incense to the goddess Guanyin every day.' He had met her at the gate of the university. 'She was so nice to me, and even asked where Professor Julian had spent his vacation.'

Julian returned to his bedroom with a cup of tea in his hand. He had begun to drink as much tea as the Chinese did, and liked its lighter flavour. English preferences like Darjeeling were spicy by comparison. He really could not stand Vole. Wizard might seem shifty but that was just how he looked. Vole, on the other hand, looked honest but was always sneaking around, curious about everything.

'Damned snake!'

Julian knew enough Chinese to sack Vole and to hire a less nosy servant. But that was not practical. He needed servants who knew English, and they were such a rare species – both Vole and Wizard had been found by the university on his behalf. Everybody on campus spoke in English to him, which meant he was still only able to speak about three hundred Chinese words. He could understand a little more, but basically it was as bad as being a deaf mute.

He was confined to bed for two days after returning from Peking, utterly drained of all energy. He had thought that he was all-powerful in sexual encounters, robust and strong, able to take on any woman in bed. But he was knocked out. His symptoms were flu-like: he felt dizzy and weak, his appetite was poor and he was sleeping badly. For several nights he could only stare at the ceiling.

This Daoist Art of Love business still nagged at him. It amounted to not much more than silly superstition. His inability, he argued with himself, was due to cultural differences. It was difficult to achieve sexual compatibility across cultures. Some things just did not come easily.

He had told the servants to buy trees from the market, and they had come back with two golden-flowered prunus. It was spring now, the time to plant trees. He should walk to the garden to have a look and thank the staff. Vole liked the new saplings, saying they would counteract the bad omen of the late-flowering peach tree last year. But he had no energy to do anything except lie motionless in bed, facing the wall, with his back to the door. He wanted very much to work things out clearly in his head.

All he could think about was Lin's return, although he was painfully aware that it would not be to his home. Their houses were less than ten minutes apart, but she was not as accessible as she had been in Peking.

Her train ticket was seven days later than his – which was her arrangement. It was not in order to avoid arousing suspicion, but because, she said, she could not stand sitting on the train with him for a day and two nights, looking at him but unable to touch him. He thought that she was right, and he had also appreciated her self-control.

But his two days alone on the train and his solitary life on his return to Wuhan had made him realize how deeply involved with her he had become. The problem he faced was not the old one of how to shake off a woman, but how to push her out of his heart, where she seemed to have taken root.

His mother's letter lay on the desk. His frequent correspondence with her was resumed: he wrote twice every week at length. As before, he wrote a little every day, telling her everything, so that his letters were more like a diary. During his visit to Peking, events had moved so fast that he did not have time to recount any news in detail. Now was a good moment to look back, but he found that his intimacy with Nessa had reached its limits. There were prohibited areas. Some things had to remain private between him and another woman.

Nessa would surely be delighted with the silks that Lin had sent her, and would hang them in a prominent position in her studio so as to show everyone who came to see her. Look, he imagined her saying, Julian sent these from China, go on, touch them, don't they feel wonderful? These Oriental works of art would also serve to remind the whole Bloomsbury set of him.

He walked to the window and opened it to let in some fresh air. Lin was nowhere to be seen. He was longing for her yet afraid of seeing her, and it made him feel utterly wretched. Once she was back they could neither carry on being innocent friends as before nor enjoy the freedom of Peking. And, because of this, they could no longer put off talking about the subject they had so far avoided – they had to formalize their relationship, by divorce then by marriage, and before all that they had to make an unequivocal commitment to each other.

The only alternative was to break it off with her, but that was almost unimaginable.

The first spring flowers were in bloom, daffodils were out on the hillsides. These flowers, commonly planted tidily in English gardens, grew wild around the ponds or along creeks here in central China.

Julian had begun to suspect that Lin might have other considerations in travelling back to Wuhan separately from him. She must have a wide circle of friends within the New Moon Society in Peking. It was unthinkable for her to leave Peking without seeing them, especially during Chinese New Year, when she was expected to go visiting. He felt left out, and in one of his letters to his mother he wrote, 'Take it easy. I shan't marry. Marriage will be a great mistake.' Nessa would surely feel relieved at this, since she was constantly worried that he would rush headlong into a foolish romance that would lead to disaster. He felt he had regained his freedom in writing those few words, and his longing for Lin was less anguished.

The next day he received a letter from Mother, not commenting on his love affair – she was always glad that he was enjoying life – but on something he had almost forgotten: his essays.

He had sent his collection of three essays via his mother to Aunt Virginia and Uncle Leonard, who ran the Hogarth Press. He had included his memorial tribute to Roger Fry, his open letter to C. Day Lewis, and an essay on liberal ethics, *War and Peace: Letter to E.M. Forster*. It had been turned down by his aunt. On the phone Mother had lost her temper with Virginia and, although she had made comforting noises in her letter, he suspected that the two sisters were at odds again.

His mind drifted back to Charleston, with its huge garden. Clive was shouting where was the coffee-pot or something like that. Aunt Virginia was probably shut up in some room, writing, while Mother gardened and responded absent-mindedly to Clive's question. In his imagination he saw Duncan's lanky, shabbily dressed figure pacing up and down the path. He had a sudden fear that the apparent harmony between them was an illusion.

In her heart of hearts his aunt was jealous of her sister, particularly of Nessa's pride in him, her son. These two women, the stars at the centre of the Bloomsbury set, regarded by the British public as the most sisterly of sisters, were in fact inescapably entangled in the most human of conflicts.

As for himself, he had to face the painful truth. Although he was a highly paid lecturer in China, he was an expert in nothing. He wanted to become a new-generation Bloomsbury poet and critic. When his early poems were collected into *Winter Movement*, which had been published two years earlier, he had won a lot of encouragement and praise from friends and family. Aunt Virginia wrote two long letters, carefully commenting on each poem. But there were few published reviews.

Influenced by the intellectual atmosphere in Europe in the early 1930s, Julian naturally drifted to criticism: on art, literature and, eventually, politics. In his essays his parents' generation were his natural opponents in the debate, although it had to be admitted they did not appear to welcome critiques by their own children. But it was difficult: they left no space for posterity to say anything new, their influence was so all-pervasive. Writing prolifically when young, they had tackled all the broadest issues in their chosen fields. Their books were all 'umbrella' works, tackling such fundamental topics as Utopianism, socialism and religion.

Julian did not lose heart. You old-style liberals will be replaced, he thought. You dared to experiment with homosexuality, promiscuity, pacifism during the Great War. We, the new generation, will experience the Daoist Art of Love, and are willing to lay down our lives in the Far East for our ideals.

Nevertheless, he was hurt by the rejection of his manuscripts. He began to doubt whether he could become a Bloomsbury figure at all. Did he have an ounce of the ability of his parents and their friends? Maybe there was no longer a need for their kind of intellectual liberalism. He knew, however, that he would never turn his back on writing poetry, and had no doubt that some of it would stand the test of time.

It was the early spring of 1936, and Julian was already twenty-eight. He had just experienced the greatest joy imaginable, and his mind kept drifting back to it. But he needed to think clearly what he wanted from his relationship with Lin, as well as reconsidering the direction his life was to take. It all left him feeling adrift in a sea of confusing emotions.

Perhaps it was only because he was not used to missing a woman so much. A cold draught entered the room and he sneezed. He felt helplessly weak.

Suddenly he heard Lin's voice below. It was just after dusk but the lights had not yet been turned on. Julian was thankful that he felt a little better that day and had got out of bed. He could hear Lin's footsteps clearly on the staircase.

She seemed as natural as in the old days, and had brought some medicine after learning that he was ill. At the sight of Julian standing at the door of his room with crumpled clothes and unkempt hair and beard she ordered him to return to bed. She said she had bought a new record of classical Chinese music in Peking, *Three Variations on the Sunset Pass*. She would put it on if he lay down. He was forced to return to bed and cover himself in a blanket. Watching her bustle around tidying up his room he suddenly felt how like a family this was, his family. 'Play it for me,' he said.

Listening to the music with her he fell into the soundest sleep he had had since coming back from Peking, and was not even aware of her leaving.

He woke up very late the next morning. The sun had already risen above the roof. At some point Lin had come and prepared a lunch of soup, rice gruel and vegetables, which were all good for a patient suffering from a cold. She issued orders to the servants, who were almost obsequious in carrying them out. Her manner was entirely relaxed and she appeared concerned only with his health. She nursed him like a sister, but kept her distance. There was not even a hint in her words about what had happened between them in Peking.

Julian looked at her resentfully. Lin noticed and said, 'There is a Chinese saying: illness hits you like a landslide; but it goes away as slowly as reeling off the raw silk from a cocoon.'

What was that supposed to mean? Was it a sly dig? No, not necessarily. People from a different culture tended to read too much meaning into common sayings.

She carried on speaking: human beings had to follow their own heart. There was nothing in this world that could not be worked out satisfactorily. The Daoists stressed that genuine wisdom could only be reached with a peaceful mind, and by allowing things to take their own course.

Julian knew that all this was just a roundabout way of telling him that she could be patient. During the days since her return he had gone over and over things in his head. He was not sure whether he was punishing a woman who genuinely loved him or punishing himself. Then again, maybe she had sucked his 'yang' dry, leaving him without any sexual desire at all. Before the Peking trip it had been hard to judge whether he loved her, since he might have been blinded by his sexual urges. Now, without them, he still found it hard to work out how he felt. The only thing he was sure of was that he needed her, although this bittersweet longing was new to him and he did not know what to make of it.

When he had completely recovered, Lin alluded to their relationship for the first time. They were in the sitting room. She did not ask whether he had missed her. She said only that the seven days they had been separated had felt like seven years to her.

She stopped at this and tears welled up in her eyes. Making an enormous effort to hold them back, she turned her head away, pushing her fist into her mouth.

Julian, who had been mentally prepared for this moment for days, had difficulty in stopping himself from pulling her into his arms. Just for the time being he baulked at a resumption of their affair, even though it had made him so deliriously happy. Lin's expression told him that she loved him deeply, with a love that went beyond sexual feelings. It was a look that frightened him, since he feared making a decision that he could not go back on.

She changed the subject then, and told him that she had seen some friends after he left, and brought back from Peking her brightest dresses, since Julian liked them – those with wide sleeves, cloth buttons and silk thread hems. They were old-fashioned now, being in a 1910s style, but that did not matter if he thought they looked good.

Julian responded just as affectionately, but felt she played the game of love much better than he did.

Since the servants were not in, Lin gradually moved closer to him without actually touching him. She gazed at him with an intensity that he had never felt in anyone before. He found it intimidating.

These kind of feelings resulted in the sort of pain that meant love could descend into farce; at least that had been his experience. But where there was no love there was no romance, and there would be no more of the intense happiness he had experienced in Peking. One should love only so much, he concluded, and no more.

Then at what point should they stop? How could they both agree to stop it there?

The indecision on his face made Lin sit back; now it was her turn to look puzzled by his reaction.

Julian had finally recovered and resumed lecturing, but many of his symptoms lingered. So Lin still had reason to visit him from time to time. In deference to his feelings, she refrained from broaching the subject of their relationship. Leaving things unspoken gave them both the freedom to decide whether to continue or not. Yet paradoxically he felt unable to decide on his own. He was even thinking of writing a novel, with the self-mocking title *Hamlet in China*.

One day Lin came to his house and stood silent for a while by the table. Suddenly she said, 'If you still refuse to go and sit in the garden I shall throw the vases onto the patio.' She snatched the pair of delicate vases by the neck, and her threats made him laugh.

But she was serious, and, returning the vessels to the table with care, said, 'You know that your poor health gives me an excuse to come. But I'm worried if you are really still unwell.' She was clearly struggling to put her feelings into words.

They went into the garden and the servants served tea and cakes. The two young plum trees were bursting with life and, looking at them, Julian felt somehow comforted. Lin, however, was no longer the caring nurse. She was filled with a sort of determination. With Wizard and Vole out of the way she lowered her voice and said that they needed to formulate a plan.

He knew instantly what she meant by a 'plan'. Since nothing could force him to promise her love and marriage she had to resume an 'affair' acceptable to him. But he did not see how. His servants were ever present. They had seriously encroached on his private life, but they were indispensable. And the weather was not warm enough for them to trek into the hills.

He remained silent and waited for her to go on. She was agitated, and began to pace up and down the garden. She looked taller with her high-heeled shoes and rose-coloured dress. She looked beautiful in any dress, but rose was most flattering, especially in the sunshine. The dress, made for her before her marriage, was a little tight and clung to her figure. She looked almost frail. Finally she stopped, and, turning to him, said what she had prepared in her mind, slowly but with clarity.

Her scheme was simple but adventurous. In the morning he

should send his servants out to shop for fresh food, telling them not to come back till nine o'clock. Her husband, as the dean, had to be in his office at eight. There was then one hour of safety, and she would come to him.

As she spoke, a slow but deep blush spread across her face, not because she was ashamed but because he had rejected her. He had been deliberately cold towards her and she was finding it unbearable. She had come to his house almost immediately upon her return from Peking, thinking that the flame kindled during their time together was still alive. She had not been sure of his love, but had every reason to expect their relationship would continue to develop. Instead, it had ground to a halt. Now she was playing her last card: she was begging him to sleep with her.

Julian knew that her proposal put them on an unequal footing. He was in a foreign country and would not suffer any humiliation if they were caught, whereas the danger to Lin was far greater. It was very hard for a Chinese woman to survive as an adulteress, and with a foreign devil at that. It would mean total rejection, even by the New Moon liberals.

He was tempted to agree. Danger excited him, especially dangerous sex. But to restart the affair? He hesitated.

Lin looked away sadly and, without waiting for an answer, started to walk out of the garden towards the path that led back home. She moved so fast that he was afraid her high heels might trip her. On an impulse he shouted, 'Yes!'

She turned, and flashed him such a brilliant smile that it made him sad. Why was he being so cruel?

He slept badly that night. The evening before, he had told the servants to go out to buy some particular food and not to return till nine. As the possibility of sex neared, he began to yearn unbearably for her. His body knew Lin better than his heart. The scenes of their lovemaking in Peking played and replayed themselves in his mind, and he felt himself grow painfully hard.

He felt driven to sit up and write a letter to his mother. Previously, his letter-diary had been an outlet for his loneliness, an opportunity to put his thoughts in order. Now he tried to allay his obsession with one woman through his love for another: an attempt to dampen the fire. But he could not find the words to express what he really felt, and he ended up feeling that he was betraying his former intimacy with his mother.

Lin's suggestion that they should continue was actually an order he was in no position to resist. His long deliberation about their relationship collapsed promptly after her few words. If she wanted to continue, he had to continue.

So he gave up trying to sleep, and went to take a long bath, scrubbing himself thoroughly with hard strokes, shaving off the unsightly beard that had been growing for the last few weeks. His body was ready and he got back into bed again. He lay under the covers, naked, waiting for her. He found himself in a state of sexual anticipation even more extreme than before they had started their affair in Peking.

The night seemed to last for ever. Towards dawn he finally fell asleep.

The sound of the front door shutting quietly jolted him awake. It must be the servants going out. Or was it Lin? She had a key. If it were she it would be followed by the sound of her footsteps on the stairs. But there was no sound at all for a long time, and he fell asleep again. Then came her light tread and the creaking of the stairs.

He tried in vain to force his eyes open. He sensed that she had entered his bedroom. He rubbed his eyes; he wanted to see her beautiful body emerge from her clothes. But he was too late. Before he knew it, she had slipped fish-like under the covers with him.

She shivered. Her hair was wet with the morning dew, and her body and lips were cold. It was almost as if she had fled from the icy halls of another world to come to his bed.

He heard a ticking under the pillow and found it was Lin's watch. This really was 'stealing love', as the Chinese termed illicit sex. The early morning sun suddenly broke through the curtains and lit up the room. Hastily, urgently, they kissed, and he entered her as soon as her legs opened a little. It felt wonderfully familiar, and for a moment they were lost in the thrill of reunion. But then she had a quick look at her watch. Julian, appalled, began to lose his erection, and quickly ejaculated, without passion. Lin had plainly not reached a climax. Her watch continued to tick away like a time bomb. Glancing at it again, she got out of the bed, threw on her clothes and rushed away.

The second morning she arrived very punctually, but their lovemaking was still so tense that it felt almost businesslike. When it was over, it was only half past eight. 'There was still time,' she said looking sadly at the watch. Julian's uncharacteristic tolerance moved her, and the two of them gazed together at the light skipping of the second hand.

In the end she left early, to reduce the danger. The room became very quiet without the ticking. Julian suddenly felt that the awkwardness of their situation might be no bad thing. It might bring about a cooling on both sides, letting the affair come to a natural end.

Their lovemaking was in grotesque contrast to their time in Peking. He could recall the details of every orgasm he had had during their short time there: where they were, how it felt, Lin's endlessly varying techniques. What was left of all that now? And what, indeed, was left of that beautiful city, doomed sooner or later to fall into enemy hands?

When she walked into his room the third time, she was surprised to see him fully clothed and sitting behind his boat-shaped desk, nursing a cup of tea. His face held a look of unfeigned boredom. Lin sat on the bed, facing him, and sighed.

'Why are you sighing?'

'I'm running a great risk in coming here! This is the year of the Rat, my birth year. I was thirty-six this New Year festival, after you left Peking.'

He raised an eyebrow – although he was not at all impressed by the mystique of the twelve-year cycle of Chinese astrology, he was interested to hear that there had been an ulterior motive behind her leaving Peking after him.

'In one's birth year, one should not change one's normal sexual patterns. It might lead to disaster.' Lin was reluctant to go on. She looked embarrassed.

'God help us!' Julian laughed. What a lot of superstition! The Chinese horoscope, with each year in the cycle represented by an animal, was even more laughable than the Western one. But China was an ancient civilization. He made an effort to pay attention to what she was saying. 'Is it so serious?'

It was her mother who had told her this, said Lin, after seeing some mention of it in the *Jade Chamber Classic*. Her father, however, had kept it so well hidden when she was a child that her mother had been unable to confirm the details. In her last birth year, when she was twenty-four, Lin decided to find out the truth for herself. So she travelled to Japan, where many of the early Chinese traditions were preserved, and paid a special visit to a Shinto temple, whose abbesses were the women of a single family, generation after generation, and carried on the teaching of the Art of Love. She enquired about the prohibitions on sex in the birth year. The Abbess told her that in such a year 'abnormal' sex was strictly prohibited, while normal sex should be moderate. As for the definition of 'normal', there were different interpretations, but, evidently, for a married woman in China sex should remain within marriage.

So, Julian thought, she had also intended to put a stop to the relationship, but when she returned to Wuhan, she, like he, had found she was unable to.

The Abbess, Lin continued, also said that intercourse with a ghost during the so-called Festival of the Dead, beginning on July 15th, was most dangerous of all and would lead to certain death within three years. The way to test this, the Abbess said, was to hang a white cloth on the eastern-facing wall; the next morning it would have bloodstains on it.

'Who would try doing that?' He knew it was a silly question: the Chinese took the most esoteric practices seriously. The Abbess had apparently strongly urged Lin not to try it.

Julian stared at Lin. He had heard a great many strange things from her, some of which had been proved right here, in his bed. What should he make of this apparent threat to her safety? He would rather ignore it. He sipped his tea, blowing away in an experienced manner the tea leaves that were floating on the surface.

Lin asked, 'Do you believe it? That there are taboos governing this year for me?'

He laughed aloud. The idea of abstaining from sex with her until the Chinese New Year! 'Of course not,' he replied, although he realized he might regret what he had said, 'otherwise there would be an awful lot of people inviting death every year!'

She smiled. 'That was exactly the Abbess told me. If the people involved don't believe in the tradition, then the prohibition doesn't apply.'

'But you believe it!' Julian said.

'No, I don't believe the whole tradition. I follow only those parts I find to be useful. This is the Confucian attitude: "Respect the gods and spirits but keep your distance."'

Such a clear statement surprised him. Whether from Lin or from Confucius, it was a complicated philosophical proposition – empiricist and utilitarian, a typical British statement, which now he found to be typically Chinese.

'What if it finally turned out to be true – I mean the disaster?'

'Then I shall believe it in my next life!' Lin said. Her courage genuinely moved him, a simple love that seemed truly to defy ill fortune. He went to her and kissed her forehead. 'Time's up. Please go home now. I shall visit you in your dreams tonight. Am I allowed?'

He was observing time more closely than she, because he genuinely cared about her predicament. She stood up in silence and left. Suddenly he felt uneasy and shouted to her just as she reached the bottom of the staircase, 'I can't wait till tomorrow morning, my love. I shall miss you all day.'

This was the first time Julian had used the word 'love', even as an endearment. It stopped her in her tracks. Then she recovered herself, and gave him the sort of ironic smile more typical of him than of her.

He was still standing on the landing. Nothing in all she had said was more moving than that she had chosen a deadly love in a minatory year. His mind kept coming back to this point. This was the way in which she loved him: like a bronze vessel cast to perfection by this romantic culture.

It was spring, and the morning mist rolled up from the lake into the hills, until it was beaten back by the noonday sun and vanished into the water. Nearly all his classes were in the afternoon. Even Tuesdays, when his classes started at ten in the morning, did not interfere with their secret meetings. If that was intentional on Lin's part, he still did not know how she had achieved such an arrangement. The timetable had been decided before the last term ended, but he still believed that Lin had had a hand in it.

Almost every year since he was eighteen he had had a new girlfriend in the spring. It was as if the season drew him to seek new love. But this spring he was in no mood. And it was not because his friendship with Lin was less than a year old, and their affair even more recent. In fact, he felt they had been together for years.

On the campus there was a strike brewing. The students were

protesting against the lack of support on the part of the university president and his 'cohorts' for their anti-Japanese activities. They demanded the president's resignation. The teaching staff were showing their solidarity with the president by declaring that they would resign en masse if he went. Many of them would lose their highly paid positions if the protest succeeded. Julian's colleagues were tense as they watched developments.

Julian could relax since his post was secure, as he had a government contract. Furthermore, everyone's attention was so taken up with the crisis that no one paid any attention to him. He was normally a very sociable person, but recently, because of his affair with Lin, he had become deliberately solitary in order to draw less attention to himself.

One morning, after the servants were gone, he was waiting for the turn of the key. But the house remained silent. He thought Lin might have met an acquaintance on the way over. Suddenly the bedroom door swung open. He jumped naked out of bed, meeting Lin in the doorway. He pulled her into the room and embraced her chilled body.

He began to peel off her dress without moving from the spot. To his surprise, he found she had nothing on underneath. Perhaps it had been like this all the previous times, only he had not realized it. No wonder her skin was so cold, even after her dash uphill to his house. She had not wanted to waste a second of her time with him. She blushed when she realized she had been found out. He led her to bed. She clung naked to him. Julian saw that her pinkish-brown nipples were protruding as urgently as they had in Peking.

He noticed a strange fragrance rising from her body, which greatly excited him. His fingers slipped inside her slippery wet vagina. That morning their lovemaking was as passionate as it had been in Peking. They threw off the quilt but did not feel the cold. Not until they had finished did they cover themselves, lying entwined, with eyes closed. This time she did not look at the watch – she had not brought it.

'Your body smells different. Why didn't I notice it before?'

'It's perfume,' Lin said simply, holding him even more tightly. He bit her ear and said, 'I don't believe it.'

Lin smiled teasingly, and waited some moments before replying. She said it was a kind of musk that her mother had given her.

He still could not believe that it was just a perfume. If she had taken a musk bath before running to him, it did not explain why the fragrance was more detectable when she was sexually excited. And when the fragrance was strong, it acted like an aphrodisiac – on him, at least. The tension that had ruined their previous lovemaking was gone. Though he was still aware of the time, it no longer preyed on his mind.

She had probably not told the whole truth, but he was content to leave it there. He knew he could never fully understand.

The only thing on his mind now was his renewed obsession with her body, which obliterated everything else. He was no longer free to choose whether to go on with this affair or break it off.

The next day, as they lay contentedly together, a new idea suddenly occurred to him.

'Will we have a child?' he asked.

She was dumbstruck for a moment, and then countered, 'Do you want one?'

'Why not?'

'Then you must marry me. I thought you didn't want to talk about it.' Lin spoke with an air of resignation.

Julian did not respond immediately. Then he asked, 'Why haven't you got pregnant yet?'

'Because I don't want to bear a bastard, and a mixed-race

one at that. It could only force you into an unwilling marriage.'

Her sharpness wounded him. His original intention had been to ask why she had no children with Cheng from their eight years of marriage.

'I was only asking how you manage not to get pregnant.'

'That's my secret.' Lin smiled.

Some women forced him to withdraw before ejaculation. The withdrawal at the last moment took a great deal of will-power and often left him dissatisfied. Lin never asked for that. On the contrary, at his climax she wanted to hold every inch of him inside.

So he said, 'If you're not meant to have a child, you won't have one.'

Julian seemed to be hinting that she was infertile and Lin felt compelled to tell the truth. 'All right, another secret. I have been practising the Art of Love all along, using musk and techniques to stop the sperm meeting with the egg.' She explained that when the tip of his penis met her cervix, this was the time for her to begin to apply a technique known as 'guarding the palace' – in Chinese the womb is known as the child's palace. If she relaxed at this point, then the sperm would rush in.

Well, I like these techniques, Julian thought. The sensation of being squeezed tight was a rare pleasure.

'I didn't want to force you to marry me because I was pregnant,' Lin said. 'That wouldn't work on a person like you. You could run back to England and I have no way to chase you there. Even if I did, and forced you to marry me, you might still get tired of me very soon, since you would resent it. By then, I would have no way out but suicide.'

Julian did not want to hear any more of this sort of thing: she was accusing him of selfishness, but he was not selfish in that way – he was only different from 'normal' people in his insistence on freedom! He stopped her by saying, 'Then let's make a child and you'll see how I behave!'

He spoke with the utmost sincerity. At that moment he really wanted to marry and have children. After all, why not? The simple candour with which Lin spoke had once more overwhelmed him.

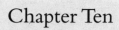

Chapter Ten

There was such harmony in their lovemaking now that they could easily synchronize their orgasm. They no longer complained about the shortage of time. Julian felt that their relationship had regained its element of freedom: it was pure sex and pure enjoyment.

One wet morning Lin looked up at the clearing sky and said that if they ever had a child it would surely be a daughter, since their lovemaking was so passionate. And she should have a beautiful name, said Lin: Hong, meaning rainbow, taken from a poem in *The Book of Songs*. The Confucian annotation to the poem was interesting: 'Rainbow: the result of intercourse between the sun and the rain. As it is improper yin-yang intercourse, it embodies the pure carnality of Heaven and Earth.' Lin wrote the Chinese character for rainbow, finishing with an elegant flourish.

'The same annotation also suggests that a rainbow in the east is seen as ominous, as a symbol of a woman running away with her illicit lover. So the rainbow is how I justify what we're doing!' She spoke with a smile, but the reference to running away was clearly not accidental.

Rainbows were frequent in this 'City of a Hundred Lakes'. During the showery seasons of spring and summer the sun would come out even before the rain stopped, and Julian, from his vantage point on Luojia Hill, would see a spectacular crescent rearing up splendidly from the hill slopes to the sky or forming an all-embracing arch.

Julian loved the imagery surrounding the rainbow. He would gaze and gaze at the sky, and dream of a daughter born of the pure but illicit sensuality between yin and yang. At this moment the world seemed as radiant to him as the vividly coloured arcs in the sky. He murmured to himself the soft sound of the word in Chinese: 'Hong…'

He grew excited and impatient, and one day asked her, 'So, any news?'

'What?' Lin was puzzled. 'Oh, you mean the child.' She went on lightly, 'Of course I'm not going to get pregnant. Not until we're ready – I mean, first we have to marry. I can't afford to let her be illegitimate, can I?'

Her bluntness angered Julian: he was not yet ready to guarantee that any child of his would have a legitimate father in the commonly accepted sense of the word. Lin knew this: she was pushing him, testing him. The conventional way of doing things had never been part of his life's experience, and he could not change now.

That day they had hardly begun to kiss before they started to quarrel.

Julian was disgusted when she did not appear to be in the mood for sex.

'All you want is…bloody…' he fumbled for the word '…yang, when *you* want it.'

'Don't be silly.' She was calm, but there was no avoiding the real issue any longer. 'If we really love each other we've got to find a solution.' She suggested that they run away to Hong Kong, to England or to America. She had sufficient savings to help him, and they could go to any corner of the world away from China. She could not go on having a clandestine affair.

What she wanted was him, the whole person, not sex by the hour.

Now she was no longer the concubine kneeling in front of the Emperor. She faced him, outfaced him, insisting on an answer. She was not going to let him off this time.

'That's impossible,' he returned. He found it easy to be cold, falling back on his reputation as a callous breaker of hearts.

Lin stood there, pale-faced and immobile. It was very simple, Julian told her. They could never be happily married. He was not prepared to contemplate marriage until he was at least forty – if he ever reached that age. And running away with him without getting married was no use to her.

'I'll go wherever you go.' She was beginning to be unreasonable. He knew that her passionate responses had often made his resistance crumble in the past, and deliberately looked away now to avoid changing his mind.

At first Lin forced a smile, but soon her composure deserted her: it was the first time she had lost her self-control in front of him. He could not bear the way her English broke down under the stress of strong emotion. Her voice began to tremble, and finally she burst into tears. There was nothing he hated more than women's hysteria. No tenderness could survive these outbursts.

She wanted to commit suicide, she said. In fact, she had had suicidal thoughts ever since her mother's death. She had not got over it until the moment when he appeared in her life. But his heartlessness had re-opened the old wound, and now thoughts of suicide had begun to recur. He was destroying her by treating their relationship as a casual affair, an adventure in which she was no more than one more alphabet letter.

'I shall take cyanide!' she declared. 'And die in front of you!'

At these words Julian flew into a rage. Had this woman been poking around in his things and seen his will? He had taken care to hide it. It was tucked inside his notebook at the bottom of his trunk, so that his secret should be revealed to nobody. Not that he had turned his back on his ambitions: he had just been unable to realize them. He tried not to look too closely into the reasons – after all, they lived in a pretty unpredictable world. But this was his problem, no one else's, and he had no intention of destroying his will.

Maybe she had not actually seen it. There was no trace of mockery on her face. Possibly it was only a coincidence: cyanide was common all over the world.

As if sensing his suspicions, Lin added, between clenched teeth, 'I can find poison. We use arsenic in China!'

She had always thought this was a good way to die, she sobbed, quick and simple, though it was cruel in that it was so final, so irreversible, there was no chance to change your mind.

If it were not for his anger at the idea that Lin might secretly have read his will, he would have laughed out loud at this. A suicide waiting to be saved? It was all so melodramatic.

Sorry, darling, you chose the wrong moment today, he said to himself. She had reminded him painfully of his will, and he was in no mood to give in to her tears or threats. He was right to freeze her out. He resolved not to budge from his position, no matter how hysterical she became. In fact, he would watch with interest to see how far she would go.

After all, he had absolutely no intention of giving up his sexual freedom. If Lin could not take his promiscuity, and was determined to stay faithful to him, well, that was her misfortune, and nothing to do with him.

He thought regretfully that no Chinese woman possessed the free spirit of Bloomsbury women. There were no Vanessa Bells, who made their husbands into friends and their friends into husbands.

For two days it rained non-stop. Julian almost fancied that the deluge from the skies was her tears. But no, God did not take sides in love affairs, Julian was not being condemned for his injustice to her. He was walking across campus in a raincoat, carrying no umbrella but wearing a wide-brimmed bamboo hat that he had bought from a peasant. When he'd dismissed the class the students had said there was going to be another storm in the afternoon. That made him feel even less like going home. The campus emptied, the wind whipped wildly at the willows and reeds at the lake's edge, forks of lightning shot out from behind the stacked-up clouds and Luojia Hill wrapped itself in swirling mists, like a particularly beautiful Chinese scroll painting.

There were several ways out: he could send a cable to Mother, 'Truth revealed', and pack for home, leaving the mess behind; or Lin and he could go public about their relationship: Lin could divorce, they would marry, and he could find work on another campus. Then again, he could stay and see whether Lin would really harm herself, and, if she did, see the truth come out, with all the teachers and students of the university accusing him. Was there a fourth way? Yes, there was, the one he had been prepared for all along.

Surely Lin could not be serious. It was only talk. But he had never been able to decide when she was telling the truth and when she was having him on. Years before he came to China he had heard Roger talk about how ordinary Chinese women regarded chastity. In every local or dynastic history there was always a long list of 'honoured chaste women' who had committed suicide to safeguard their moral purity, which was more important to them than life, or love.

Was Lin that stupid? She could not be. She was Western-educated, and also a Daoist who regarded outward appearances as deceptive and believed that the ultimate goal was health and longevity. She was only venting her anger on him for not marrying her.

Perhaps she was only putting on an act. Was everything between them only an act? It was hard to tell truth from fantasy in China – at least *he* found it hard.

He saw Cheng coming his way with an umbrella. He was thinner than before. They greeted each other and stopped to exchange a few words. He was one of the two people, together with Lin, that Julian least wanted to see at that moment. But Cheng seemed quite unaware of anything unusual going on. He was as polite as ever, even more so as he was in a hurry. He turned back just after striding off, to tell Julian that he had been greatly impressed by his poems and essay and urging him to come and visit them, any time he wanted.

Julian warmed to him. He had given Lin a copy of his poetry collection, *Winter Movement*, and part of his essay on Roger Fry had been mimeographed by the secretaries' office and used as reading material for the students. Cheng really was a good man, and a scholar, too – what was more, he was always nice to him.

He felt some compunction at deceiving someone so innocent. What if one day Cheng came to know of Julian's affair with his wife? What a blow to his dignity and his reputation that would be. But he reassured himself that Cheng was too intelligent to kick up too much of a fuss.

Julian stood in the drizzling rain, unable to make up his mind whether to tell Cheng the truth or to go on cheating, waiting for him to discover it one day.

He left the campus and called a rickshaw to go to Hankou. He needed a break from the stifling atmosphere of the university, riddled as it was with gossip and conspiracy. The envelope of one of his mother's letters had looked strange. Lin said that it might have been opened by an 'enemy' of Cheng's. This made him furious: there was little enough privacy as it was. It was all right for the Chinese to hate each other, since there were so many of them. But what juicy revelations might they have gleaned from his mother's letter?

He crossed the Yangtze to the north bank, landing in the former British settlement. To the east was the celebrated Carved Buildings Street, with its teahouses, wine-houses and other stores and shops all built with wood. Every inch of every building seemed to be covered with delicate reliefs of birds and flowers, mountains and rivers, and the arch at the street entrance was magnificently decorated.

By the time Julian had had his fill of wandering around the area, and enjoyed a good meal with wine, darkness had already fallen. He went to the ferry pier. The rain was unrelenting and the raindrops made tiny flower-like patterns on the choppy water. He looked at his watch unsteadily. Half past six, or was it quarter to seven? He was drunk.

He asked a policeman standing nearby: '*Zouma*? Is anyone leaving?' His Chinese pronunciation always sounded perfect to him when he was drunk.

'*Shenme*?' The policeman clearly did not understand.

'The ferry boat!'

'*Meiyou! Meiyou!*' The answer was negative.

The wind had strengthened without warning, as if from nowhere, and now it all but blew his bamboo hat off. He had to press it down while his raincoat fluttered madly. All those carrying umbrellas were caught in a struggle between saving the umbrella and protecting themselves from the rain.

The ferry service was suspended. Julian had no choice but to go to the waiting hall, which he found intolerably filthy, crowded with stranded passengers. The ground was covered with spittle, the air filled with a suffocating blend of men's sweat, children's urine and women swearing. He found it strange that he only noticed the wretchedness of China when he was not with Lin.

It was a further two hours before the ferry slowly chugged away from the pier. Once the river breeze had cleared his head of alcohol there was only the pain left, and his head was now heavy and aching. He was badly in need of another glass of brandy.

All the same, he did not go directly home but passed via Lin's house where he paused under a locust tree. The lamp with the Japanese shade was shining in the sitting room, but only Cheng was there, reading. Lin's room upstairs was dark. What was he doing here, standing drunk in the rain? Julian berated himself for acting like a lovesick fool. There was nothing untoward in the appearance of the house. Well then, she must be alive. There was no point in going on watching, he told himself angrily, and set off for home.

She had not come for several days now. He felt an unaccustomed emptiness in his life, and did not know what to do with himself. Her absence, his inability to see her, left him desolate.

Ten minutes to his own house. He tried to take the route Lin used every morning. He doubted whether she was as miserable as he was now. She had come every morning, her dress fluttering around her naked body, through the bamboo groves, pushing aside leafy branches. She probably ran in order to have a few more minutes with him. The path was steep, and slippery after the rain. How did she manage it without arriving completely out of breath, as he was now? And she never complained – never once mentioned the difficult climb.

Once home, the two servants came to take his raincoat and bamboo hat and waited on him solicitously. 'Should I make you something for your hangover, sir?' asked Wizard.

Julian was sitting slumped in his armchair. He shook his head and said he needed a brandy.

'Anything else, sir?' Vole asked.

'Just don't bother me!' Julian suddenly lost his temper and shouted, which he had never done before. The British always made it a point to be polite, if patronizing, to the household staff.

This was madness! Perhaps he'd better buy that bottle of cyanide. Or die in her arms, with no need for the cyanide. Just let her use her Daoist arts on him. She had spent plenty of time rehearsing them in private. Let him die exhausted, all passion spent, just like the sex-crazed hero in *The Golden Lotus*.

At the thought, he began to laugh, startling the two servants, who were outside the door. It was ridiculous to contemplate sacrificing his life for a Chinese woman, even if she was beautiful and talented, and a witch in bed!

The following day he made a point of leaving his house early, at a quarter to eight, before Lin could possibly get there. His class did not start till ten o'clock, so he went to his office in the department of English. In the corridor he bumped into two women. They introduced themselves as the new language teachers in his department. One was English and the other American. Both had husbands working in companies in Hankou – men who travelled frequently. They had nothing to do at home, so they had come to be temporary English teachers, to pass the time, as they put it.

Julian's spirits rose. His affair with Lin had left him friendless, with neither the time nor the inclination to meet new people. After all, he did not want to draw attention to himself. But he was sociable by nature, and when he travelled in Europe, even with a girlfriend, he was always to be found in a crowd.

Now he was in the company of two young women. Whether or not they were truly beautiful did not matter, since they both had the undeniable attraction of youth. The old excitement of getting to know a new woman came back to him. He set out to be witty and amusing. The two women were able to flirt openly, since they were as good as single and free. Within a few minutes they had invited him to take them out for meals, and separately at that. They meant it as a joke but it was exactly what he wanted.

After his class that day Julian invited the English woman for lunch and the American for dinner. They talked the same language and the conversation flowed. The flirting was easy, the innuendo delicate and there were no awkward misunderstandings.

That American was more interested in politics, or said she was. From their seats in the Wuchang restaurant they had an unimpeded view of the lights of Hankou on the north bank of the Yangtze River.

She asked whether there were any underground Communists on campus.

Julian did not answer directly. In fact, he had thought it better not to try to find out. There might be quite a number of students who held more or less Marxist views. When he had tried to discuss a Marxist analysis of Dostoevsky the faces in front of him looked tense and anxious, which he found interesting. From this he gauged that the leftwing students were scared he might say something offensive to Marxism, which would leave them with no choice but to stand up and argue back – not a very comfortable thing for a Chinese student to do.

The food and wine were good, and they were enjoying them. Julian had become quite a gourmet in China, and was glad to show off his knowledge to this American. They chatted about Bloomsbury and the crisis in Europe. Julian refused to believe that it would engulf China.

He also spoke a little about politics. Several columns of the Red Army, he said, were under pressure to retreat to a desolate area of western China, and the police in Peking had raided some major universities and arrested radical students and professors. For both these reasons a strike was quite likely on this campus.

Julian raised his glass and said to the woman, 'Drink it down, as the Chinese say.' He drank the whole glass down in one go. 'To the strike, if nothing else.'

The American woman was attractively flushed after draining her wine. She pulled her chair a little closer to Julian and asked, 'If there's a strike, how would you spend your time?'

'Making love,' Julian replied without even thinking about it.

She stared at him, shocked. Julian stared back. He enjoyed making provocative comments and then staring challengingly at the woman to see her reaction. Her face flushed a fiery red and she looked away. He smiled. He felt as if he were back in Europe. He used to be good at this kind of conquest, and good, too, at dumping those he no longer wanted.

So he went on. 'If there's no strike I shall start to lecture on the Cambridge liberal thinkers, from G.E. Moore to Bertie

Russell, not in detail, but enough to encourage the students to think about the principles of liberalism.' He was a far more confident teacher now, after his months of practice.

The American sighed. She knew little about these things, and was bored. 'Very interesting,' she said. No, he didn't want to go to bed with her, he thought, not tonight. And tomorrow was another day. He was perfectly in command of the situation.

He felt much more cheerful. He had meals with one or other of the two women, even inviting each of them to his house for dinner. Both pretended not to care, though they shared an intense rivalry for his attentions. It pleased him to stroll around the campus with one or other of them. The Chinese did not care much about what the European men and women got up to, and he could flirt openly, which he loved to do.

Then it began to pall. He called a halt before sleeping with either of them.

One day, when he was on his way to a class, he found Lin waiting for him on the road. She looked like a student again, in her white cotton dress and cloth shoes with no make-up, in total contrast to her glamorous outfits in Peking. Her hair was caught up into two pigtails. But her face was bony and she looked very thin.

He had expected the meeting, yet he was put out at being ambushed in this way. 'Still in the land of the living, I see...' As soon as the words were out of his mouth he realized he had been cracking too many jokes recently. It was only too easy to be cruel.

Lin did not seem to hear. She started with the words she had prepared.

'I hear you have now had L and M. Congratulations!'

'Nonsense!' he said, almost instinctively, though he had mentally decided that he would not deny it if she asked him about it.

She smiled and moved closer. 'You don't have to lie. You are handsome, attractive, charming. You come from a famous family. You are a young professor and thinker, a gifted poet. How could any woman not fall in love with you?'

She didn't seem to be accusing him. Nor was there any note of irony in her voice. She must have been feeling wronged: the man she loved was humiliating her. Seeing the tears in her eyes, he felt torn. She was apparently trying hard to control herself, and told him that she blamed herself for falling in love with the wrong man, and for not being able to forget him. She gradually moved closer to him, and her eyes had a wild, reckless look.

'Don't, please.' Julian could hardly bear the way she looked at him, and turned his face away.

'You would rather see me die, wouldn't you?' Her sigh broke his heart. 'I will, when the time comes. But please, Julian, I beg you. Don't throw me aside like this.'

'I'm not.' He didn't know what he was denying – abandoning her or wanting to see her die.

Her eyes had lost their shine now, and her breathing was shallow. He suddenly realized that love was the stuff of life itself to her, that she might really have been thinking of suicide – God alone knew whether she had a 'self-termination method' like she had a method for everything else in their relationship. She had said repeatedly, 'dying in front of you'. He knew he had degraded her, and himself, too, by going out with two women for whom he felt nothing.

Suddenly he felt indescribably guilty, and pulled her against him, holding her tight.

'I love you.' This was the first time he had said this to her; it shocked him as much as her. And he added, 'Believe me, please.'

Lin was stupefied, and her breath came a little faster. Then she helplessly shook her head. 'I know I'm cheap. I used the threat of suicide to force you into this. I know you really feel for my predicament. That should be enough for me.'

She raised her head. A little colour returned to her face, as if her spirits had revived. 'My mother always said that to be prepared to cheapen oneself can be the noblest option.' She shook herself free and asked Julian to walk away first.

After a dozen paces he turned his head, but Lin was nowhere to be seen. He went on, lost in thought, until all that he could hear were the raucous cries of invisible birds and the screams of the monkeys.

He discovered that he had actually been walking in the wrong direction, away from the campus, and was now lost in the dense forest amongst a mass of azaleas and morning glory flowers, with their large and brilliant trumpets. Thin rays of bright sunlight pierced the gloomy undergrowth.

He put his hands over his ears to block out the din of the forest and made an effort to calm down. Once he had managed to reorientate himself he headed back to the campus. He was forty minutes late for class. The students were worried and had sent people to search for him in his office and home, and when they could not find him they had gone to the dean's office.

His apology to the class was matter of fact. 'Sorry, I lost my way.' He said it so earnestly that he began to laugh at himself, and the students laughed too.

The whole day seemed unreal. He had a dinner date with the English woman; it was her invitation. He did not want to go but it was too late to call it off. So he returned home to put on a suit and tie, and carefully combed his hair before he went. He had never dressed so elaborately to see Lin.

The English woman was overdressed too. She wore a cheongsam, for God's sake, and a pearl necklace, and the result made her look like a Chinese cigarette advertisement. To cap it all she wore two very red roses in her hair: the effect was slightly comic, like an actress back home playing one of Somerset Maugham's Chinese characters.

'You look a little distracted,' she noticed immediately.

Julian apologized, saying that he had been in the hills and caught a chill.

She was flattered – it was nice, she said, that he had come even when he was not feeling well. The happier she was, the sadder he became; it made him feel that European women were insensitive. If it were Lin, she would have forced him to go home to bed. Also, cheongsams, with their high side slits, just did not look right on the European figure: they had been designed to complement the shape of Chinese women.

He could hardly bring himself to look at her, and turned his gaze towards the door. Just then he saw the American woman coming in with a European man. So she was not wasting any time moping over him. The same would be true, he thought cynically, of this rose-bedecked woman sitting opposite him, should he not be available.

I am being too hard on them, he thought. I'm just in a foul mood. After all, I'm playing the same game as them, and we don't owe each other anything.

He did his best to keep his partner amused, but he found it hard to get his dinner down. What a chatterbox she was. As soon as they had finished the dessert he called a taxi to take her home.

Once in the taxi she insisted that since Julian was not well he should be dropped off home first. He did not demur. At the door he planted a good night kiss on her cheek and, without further ado, went inside and shut the door.

He went to his bedroom feeling tormented. Perhaps some Chinese music would lull him to sleep.

The evocative sounds filled the room: a cascade of water, the chimes of a wooden percussion instrument, a bronze temple bell, the sighing of the wind in the trees.

He began to dream vividly. The skylarks are singing, and a pebble drops into a pond. He is not surprised when a Chinese woman, with hair piled high on her head, in an ancient court dress and glittering jewellery, walks out of the bamboo grove into his bedroom. He has seen her before somewhere. She is flawlessly beautiful, even through the tear stains on her face.

He tries in vain to extricate himself from the bedclothes. In the middle of the room she starts to undress, each layer of clothing falling from her like the ages of history. As she does this her appearance alters imperceptibly.

He is bewitched by her performance, but then she begins to chant her words of accusation.

'You fear love and hurt the one who loves you. Do not wait too long. The time will come when you realize, too late, that you cannot live without love. Reject me and you reject yourself, since I am already part of your life.

'I am a virgin. I renew my virginity again and again. And each love is like my first love. Now you see I have one last layer of clothing. I am a modern woman now. Once I remove this, I shall be pure womanhood.

'Are you capable of showing me your love?'

Now she is naked and lying on him, wriggling like a snake, entwining herself around his cock. He cannot control himself and ejaculates prematurely. She is furious and slaps him violently in the face. But the pain is nothing in comparison with the contempt he sees on her face.

She leaves him and goes to lie on his desk. Her voice now comes as a gentle song. 'When that which goes has gone, how can that which remains stay?'

And the desk floats like a boat out of the window. He rushes to look out, but it has flown.

The sound of his own voice awoke him. It was three o'clock in the morning. Every cell in his body felt wide awake. He remembered every detail of his dream, although he was unable to make sense of it.

The gramophone that had not been played for so long, the

swirling fabrics hanging on the wall, the two china vases and the delicately carved furniture, every thing of beauty in his world was connected with her. Without her, the world was not complete: it lacked its essential truth.

He had always known this. He was now more aware of it than ever. I always destroy what I love most. Her suffering causes me such pain. Why am I doing this to myself? What am I frightened of? I am making us both miserable.

Julian tried to find his yellow handkerchief, the gift she had given him with the initial K on it. It was nowhere to be found. He searched frantically until finally, exhausted, he sat down at the top of the stairs.

He had to give up looking. Everything comes and goes as it will. Why force something to happen? Daoism again. The handkerchief would surely turn up when he least expected it.

Julian sent his servants out shopping early the next morning. He waited for eight o'clock, wondering if she would come. Well, it was a quarter past eight now, and the door remained closed. There were no footsteps. So he would go down to meet her.

He walked to her house. Taking the downhill path in leaps and bounds, it took only eight minutes. Lin was sitting on her doorstep as if waiting for him. The sun was rising behind the trees on the hill and enveloped both of them in its brightness. They saw each other and said, simultaneously, 'I had a dream.' Surprised, both of them stopped.

Had they shared the same dream? What if she repeated it now and gave him a slap in the face? That might be a good thing for both of them, he thought. He wanted desperately to apologize for everything, inside or outside the dream, and to take her back to his house now, so that they could try to make amends.

He was about to say it when the door behind Lin creaked. Out walked a young Chinese man, tall, strong and well proportioned, in a spotless creamy white suit, smart tie and leather shoes. Julian considered himself better-looking than most Chinese men, but now he saw someone who was undeniably more attractive than him.

The young man nodded perfunctorily to Julian, took Lin's arm and walked away with her. Julian felt his anger flare up. The man had not even taken the trouble to greet him. A new lover! Someone from the New Moon Society? The way they walked arm in arm suggested a long and intimate relationship. A virgin again and again, she had said in his dream – what a lie!

His head was spinning; he did not know what to make of it. He even pictured Lin naked in the man's arms, and he, the man, slipping in between her legs.

He rushed back to the university library, half hoping to find them, then on to the department. It was too early for his class. By chance he bumped into Cheng on the stairs. As usual they exchanged a few words. Without even thinking, Julian told him that he had seen Lin with a handsome stranger, who seemed on unusually intimate terms with her.

'That's Lin's brother, just returned from America. He is passing through Wuhan. Should I introduce him to you?'

Her brother! Her father had had so many concubines she must have a whole squadron of siblings. Julian tried to pass off his indiscretion with a laugh. 'It would be nice to meet him. A good-looking young man always catches my attention, I'm afraid. We're like that in my family.'

But the incident continued to weigh on him. He knew that his reaction had been despicable. He should be ashamed of himself. Had it not been Lin's brother, what might have been the consequences of his words to Cheng? What was he doing spying and informing on her like this? What a bastard he was!

He genuinely regretted his behaviour.

'Everything here is like a bad novel.' Those were the words written by his father Clive to Aunt Virginia many years ago, just before Julian was born. Looking back with the advantage of hindsight, he could see the continuing strains in the relationship between his father, mother and aunt. Their liberal reputation, and their position among the cultural elite of British society, had made their lives public property. And now they were forced to continue practising the principles of remarkable frankness and freedom they had espoused. But the seeds of resentment had been planted long ago, and whenever the opportunity arose they would take revenge on each other. For instance, when Aunt Virginia refused to publish his essays.

Chapter Eleven

The next morning Julian lay in bed, waiting. Would she come? He wasn't sure. If she did come, they could have a healthy laugh to put all their misunderstandings behind them. After the servants had left he heard a light click at the door and someone coming in, followed by the sound of the door closing. He waited for her footsteps on the stairs. In the quiet of the early morning those light steps struck his ears as sweeter than birdsong. Yes, it must be her.

The house was quiet, utterly quiet. There was no sound for a long while.

He could wait no longer, and ran downstairs without even stopping to throw on some clothes. There was no one there. Then he saw an envelope addressed to him on the table by a potted plant. He opened it. There was a small notebook inside and a key. His key! It was the key he had given her at the beginning. She *had* been here. Her fragrance hung in the air, he could smell it. She had given him back the key as a way of telling him she had come for the last time.

'But I told her I loved her, didn't I?' He almost yelped with frustration.

Why were Chinese women so difficult to handle? Maybe it was for the best – for both of them. She had had enough of love affairs. Maybe he had too. Suddenly he found that his interest in those other two women had evaporated.

He remembered there was a reception that evening at the British consulate in Wuhan. Since his arrival in China, Julian had done his best to avoid having anything to do with officialdom. He knew the consulate was probably keeping an eye on him as a result of the student demonstration when he had been injured.

But the business with Lin was upsetting him badly, and now he came to think about it it would be a good idea to make an appearance there in person.

He got dressed and put the key in the pocket of his jacket. It was then that he realized that the notebook contained Lin's hand-written poems. She had told him in Peking that she also wrote poetry, but it was more for herself than for others, and had not achieved the recognition of her novels.

'I'd love to read them.'

'No, not now… Maybe one day,' she had replied evasively. 'It's because…'

'Because they are about me?' He hazarded a guess.

She shook her head in silence.

'Is that a yes or a no?'

'Neither.' And she had looked away, suddenly lost in thought

So why should she give him her poems now? Was it just another riddle? He leafed through the little notebook. The poems were all written in neat Chinese brushstrokes, with only one that she had tried translating into English. There was no title. He read with great curiosity:

Apart from the rain, there is only a tearing open.
In the north, the page of a letter is spiked on an iron fence
Wings tightly furled. Three times, three times it tries to fly, but
cannot.

A wild storm blazes in your heart.
At the roadside you meet a woman, who lowers her eyes.

Julian was surprised that modern Chinese poetry could be like this. The lines were limpidly clear, yet darkly pregnant with meaning. The poem was obviously about him, about the anguish of loving him, yet the pain was made more poignant through understatement. This was typical of classical Chinese poetry. By comparison, his own poems were clumsy, full of convoluted syntax and densely woven metaphors.

Strange that he had judged modern Chinese poetry, from his reading of only a few poor translations, as just a pale imitation of Western romantic poetry. Clearly he had been too hasty.

Could she be a better poet than he was?

The thought struck at his self-esteem. If he lost out to her in their lovemaking he could dismiss the Art of Love as just a Chinese game. But if she beat him at poetry, well, that was *his* game.

He had to acknowledge now that he had nothing to be smug about in her presence – she was quite simply a more gifted writer. The only difference was that his mother tongue was English, and he had read more European literature than her, while she wrote in Chinese and was deeply immersed in Chinese culture. His only advantage was the one given to him by his language.

Julian felt suddenly and painfully that his career had now reached a dead end. He had always seen himself as a poet and believed that some of his work would be passed down to posterity. Now he began to doubt this. He had been the golden boy of the Bloomsbury set; did he really have nothing in the way of talent or expertise? What could he hope to achieve in life?

Julian had a new servant who, although he had no English, cooked much better than Wizard and Vole. He had been sent to him by Lin. Unlike most other cooks he was extremely skinny; he also managed to get on well with the old servants. In fact, they were delighted with him since they now had less work to do.

Julian calmed down, returned to his bedroom and sat down at his desk. In his drawer he found a translation of one of Lin's stories: 'Temptation'. She had given it to him long ago and he had sent a copy to Mother, together with a note. 'I am sending you Lin's story. I hope it should force you to write to me more often.'

The story was about a couple entertaining a visitor. At the end of the evening the guest went to sleep on the couch. The wife was filled with an overwhelming desire to kiss him. The husband was angry, but in the end gave his permission. Upon which the wife, quite inexplicably, lost the wish to do it.

Julian had to admit this was an excellent piece of work, written in a light, elegant vein quite unlike the moralistic tones of contemporary Chinese literature. Lin had given it to him on her return from Peking.

'I hope you can manage to have the story published in England,' he had written. If that happened, Lin would be very happy. He would do it to please her. Lin had not asked him to get it published, and at this moment he could not talk to her about it. Please don't hate me, he mentally addressed her; try to understand me. I know you think I'm a cold fish, but I'm not. People just have different ways of expressing their love.

At the gate of the Hotel Oriens Extremus, 897 Dr Sun Yat-Sen Boulevard in Hankou, sedan cars and taxis lined up to unload their passengers. The five-storey hotel, with its balconies on all sides, had been built not long before the British settlement was taken over by the Chinese. It was still the most luxurious hotel in Wuhan, and this evening the hall was full of men in tuxedos and women in evening dresses.

Buoyed up by the grandeur of the occasion, everyone was in good spirits. The British consulate had invited not only foreign diplomats and notable businessmen but also the cream of Wuhan Chinese society. There were three or four hundred people there, three-quarters of them Westerners. Julian arrived when the party was in full swing. He saw a few well-known professors from the university. Waiters in white jackets and bow-ties were carrying trays with wine and snacks for the guests.

Julian was offered red or white wine or champagne, and began to feel as if he were back in London society. He was extremely thirsty and downed several glasses of whatever was on offer, beginning to get into the mood of the evening. Soon he was beaming with suave confidence, although in London he had always despised such social gatherings as vulgar.

Most of the women were overdressed and he dismissed them with a glance. Beautiful women were too damned scarce. None of the Western women was anything special, and the Chinese ones were only passable. Against the background of flowers and lamps, Julian saw himself reflected in a huge mirror with a gilt frame: a tall young man in a bow-tie and well-fitting suit, he stood out from the other European men.

The band, made up of Westerners and Chinese, was quite large. Their music was not brilliant but the atmosphere was good. The floor was swirling with dancers. He spotted an extremely attractive woman and his eyes lingered on her. Then she turned, and with a start he saw it was Lin. Her dress, which he at first took for white, was in fact lilac. A lilac so pale that you had to look closely to see its true colour. Her hair was piled high at the back of her head, exposing her neck and long pendant earrings. She wore a sleeveless, tight-fitting gown and her arms were covered by matching silk gloves to the elbows. She looked stunning.

What was she doing here? Wherever he went, she got there before him! But it must just be coincidence. He had not seen her for several days. The reception at the British consulate was an important social event, and it was natural for her to be invited – she was a well-known writer, after all.

It was the first time he had seen Lin in Western dress, wearing make-up, too: it made her look like a new woman. She did not have glasses on. He remembered telling her that she looked better without them when she went out, but he had meant when they were together.

She seemed in good spirits and looked extraordinarily

charming as she talked and laughed with her dancing partner, a good-looking blond fellow.

As soon as the music finished, Julian approached and politely took her arm, casually excusing himself to her partner. Lin seemed surprised to see him, but quickly recovered herself, and, as naturally as if she had been waiting to dance with him, raised her hand to his shoulder. The neckline of her dress was cut away, exposing her rounded shoulders. He caught sight of her smooth armpits and suddenly felt hot with desire.

They held hands and his arm encircled her waist. She looked down at first, but continued to smile. She was a good and graceful dancer, obviously no stranger to this kind of occasion.

Finally she raised her head. Thank you, music! thought Julian. She looked at him with the old familiar look of love, a moist, hot look. He clasped her tighter and she yielded. He knew now that she still loved him, that she had always loved him. All his resentment and anger evaporated. He searched his pocket and found the key still there. He took it out and slipped it into her hand. Their movements were so natural that no one could have noticed. Lin looked at him and smiled, and he smiled back. Then suddenly he thought of Cheng, that Cheng might be watching them, and his smile froze on his lips.

At that moment the music stopped. They walked to a sofa at the edge of the dancefloor. He looked around. Cheng had not come. The college students' demands were becoming more strident. Many classes had already stopped. Negotiations were getting nowhere and, as one of the university deans, Cheng was probably too involved to be in the mood for a party. However, the English language teacher whom Lin had called L was there, actually walking towards them. Lin, who knew so many people, recognized her too. Lin borrowed a pen from someone and wrote on his palm three Chinese characters, of which he could recognize only the first: *bu*, meaning 'not'.

'Not jealous,' she translated in a low voice. But who should not be jealous of whom? She must mean that she was not jealous.

Fine. So she was not jealous, then.

A man on the neighbouring couch gave up his seat for Lin. She thanked him and sat down. How changed she was, talking and laughing amongst friends and acquaintances. He knew that Lin was playing with fire, the fire of his feelings. The flames began to devour him. Talking with L, he gazed deep into her eyes and flirted outrageously with her, something he could do effortlessly. But Lin never even glanced in his direction. She had always had better self-control than he.

The French windows stretched from floor to ceiling. Through the open ones the lights of the opposite bank were visible, while the closed ones reflected the chandeliers, the flowers and the crowds of people.

When it was the time for dinner they found themselves seated at the same long table but quite a distance apart. Julian began to feel disheartened. Lin never looked at him, and carried on charming her neighbours. He had no appetite and only nibbled a little at the first two courses. His attention was completely concentrated on Lin. The waiters passed with the dessert, vanilla ice-cream topped with a strawberry. He could not touch it. The greater the gaiety around him, the more miserable he felt. He excused himself and went home alone.

He left the three characters, 'not jealous', on his hand for a day before he washed it. Now he could write them. The word 'jealous' was made up of two Chinese characters, each with a component that, on its own, also meant 'woman'. Its curve, soft and graceful, seemed more significant than the meaning of the word. He gazed at the message.

The Chinese characters containing this woman component were either very negative words or very positive, with almost none in between. But he still could not understand who was supposed not to be jealous of whom. He looked at the characters and seemed to see the woman components start to sway provocatively. Each Chinese character, it seemed, had an anima in it. When the common people in China burned paper on the streets they separated out the paper with words on and kowtowed before setting it alight.

He recalled Ezra Pound's theory of 'ideogrammatic poetics', and his poems with Chinese characters embedded in them. He used to think the man was an eccentric windbag, but now suspected he might actually be a genius, with an instinct for the poetic potential of the Chinese language.

He was sure Lin would not come, but he still sent the servants out shopping early, just in case. Julian realized that he craved her with a passion that their little hour of happiness could not satisfy. It was not simply a physical need. In his dream she had said, 'When that which goes has gone, how can that which remains stay?' That was esoteric, too hard to fathom. If Lin made use of his key she would once again open the floodgates of his feelings; if she did not, then how could he persuade her to try again?

By accepting her demands, of course, but to what extent?

Not only did she stay away, she dropped off the horizon, from the classroom, from the campus. In his letter to his mother that week, he wrote as usual about numerous things in his life, while there was only one short sentence about Lin: 'The affair appears to have ended.'

In fact, he was miserable. It was May, the season of blossom and of burgeoning growth; it was all in grotesque contrast to the desolation in his heart.

He was immensely irritated with himself. There are so many beautiful Chinese women. What's to stop me finding a new mistress? Why must it be Lin and no one else?

He went to her house. It was Sunday, when both Lin and Cheng ought to be at home. He knocked at their door, and the servant announced him: 'Professor Bell.'

Cheng came out to welcome him, and the servant brought them tea. Julian said that there was nothing important: he had bought some ceramics and a painting. He hoped Mrs Dean would be so kind as to help determine whether they were forgeries.

Everything in the drawing room was the same. But the flowers were now white, though he vaguely remembered that Lin did not like white flowers. He also noticed there was a new picture on the mantelpiece: beside the one with Tagore there was one taken by a photographer on the evening his department colleagues had welcomed him. He looked a little nervous, but apparently happy, at the centre of the snapshot. Lin was standing closest to him. It was quite natural for her to place that photo in the drawing room. But to him it said that she still wanted him.

Cheng said, 'Lin's not in. She goes into town every day.'

'To Hankou?' he asked.

'A few writers and poets from the north – all old friends – are paying a visit and she's taking them around since she's the editor of the *Wuhan Daily Literary Supplement*. She has taken them to the park, to the Zither Terrace on Snake Hill, and I think today they went to see the Five Hundred Arhats of the Buddhist Temple.'

Julian left without finishing his tea.

No, he was not jealous. If Lin did not come, it was through her own free will. He tried to persuade himself it was a good sign. It meant that she was not suicidal. And why indeed should she be? She had her own life and enjoyed her reputation among the Chinese literati. He remembered again her poems, her ability, her education and her wealthy family background – she was better at everything than he was. He was not even a worthy opponent in bed! Of course she was not going to come pleading for his love.

She had been stunning at the party that evening. The more captivating she was, the more she ensnared him. And now she was out every day with her guests, amongst whom he had no place, and had not even bothered to let him know. Her need to love him seemed to have evaporated.

And Chinese literary circles! When he flirted with the two women in his department he had understood what a difference it made to do so in one's mother tongue rather than an acquired language! So now Lin was among her Chinese-speaking colleagues and friends, and she must be very much at home.

'Not jealous.' He was surprised to find he could not help being jealous. And he was not just jealous, he was desperately so.

He wrote the three characters on his hand again. They were soon smudged by his sweat. How he wished Lin would appear on the little path to his house and, once inside, appear naked before him as if by magic. He closed his eyes in longing. Their daily early morning lovemaking had been as full of anguish as of happiness, but now he would give anything to turn back the clock.

★

One thing about Hankou was very different from the campus on Luojia Hill. When evening came and darkness fell over the city, the neon-lit streets came alive. Teahouses, restaurants, bars, brothels, theatres were full of people looking for pleasure.

The noise of drums and singing filled his ears. There was a large crowd in front of him. Standing on tiptoe, he could just see over their heads what was happening: it was a group of street performers singing and dancing, each adorned with red dots on their cheeks and lips, carrying flowered handkerchiefs and fans, led by a woman. The noise of the drums was deafening.

Julian turned right and entered the Imperial Red House. He

went up to the bar. The young White Russian woman called Anna was serving. After a whisky, he told her he had come to learn the tango. She was happy to teach him, and took him onto the dancefloor. He was not too familiar with the complicated steps, but managed to follow her movements. The tango was basically a dance of seduction, of the body's advance and retreat, and he became intoxicated with their rhythmic movements. When Anna leaned invitingly against him in the course of the dance, he bent over her and their eyes met.

She took him to her home, a small room on the second floor of a hotel not far from the bar, and to bed. When they were finished, and Julian started to put on his clothes, she sat up in bed and asked whether he would stay the night.

Julian thanked her with a kiss on the forehead and promised that he would come again.

He stuffed a few banknotes under the pillow to avoid the embarrassment of paying into her hand. She tried not to notice. Of course he would not come again. It was not that the hotel was run-down and her roomy dingy – though at least the bed was clean enough. It was just that this sort of sexual release left him feeling uncomfortable, disgusted with himself.

It was very dark outside. A heat haze hung over the city, and only a cool evening breeze brought some relief. The streets were thronged. Rickshaw men offered their services but Julian preferred to walk on alone.

Anna was a typical White Russian, with her plump breasts, rounded hips and coquettish manner, and she knew how to please a man in bed. But he kept his eyes closed while he was doing it. In his mind he was seeing Lin's sweet body, and at the moment of ejaculation he almost called her name. Anna's body was stocky, with abundant hair at her pubis and under her armpits, which smelt faintly sour. Her skin felt coarse to him, and her back was covered in spots. Yet she was no worse than many other Western women. His memory had faded in the last year. They were a little better when young, but past thirty their charm was gone for ever.

He forced himself to stop seeing Lin's silken skin, her body with its mysterious fragrance. The more he thought, the more pitiful he appeared to himself. He had fallen almost as low as the White Russian woman.

No, he would not give this one an alphabet letter, not even after going to bed with her. After Lin, he could never give any woman a letter again. This time he had paid money to erase the memory.

Now he had an idea of what Lin meant. 'Not jealous' meant he should not be jealous. He had, in fact, let Lin turn the tables on him. He had come to China to receive a basic lesson in liberalism!

'Fuck you!'

He almost howled it. But who was he cursing? Lin? Himself? He was just an abject failure with no job, no prospects and no one to love him.

He stared dully at the opposite bank of the river. Luojia Hill was completely enveloped in a haze so dense it even blotted out the street lights. He suddenly remembered that the yellow handkerchief was tucked in between all the letters from Mother. He laughed, remembering how desperately he had looked for it. How futile it had been to try so hard to find it. It had simply turned up in the course of time.

He discovered that he had reached the door of the Imperial Red House again. It sounded rowdy inside, and he sensed a tension in the air. It was busier than usual. People were talking heatedly and knocking back glasses of brandy. He ordered one himself, and asked the bartender what was going on. News had broken of the Spanish Civil War, with Germany and Italy supporting one side and Russia the other.

His heart gave a thud. Maybe some of his British friends

would join up. When he had left Europe, Fascism was already a threat, and war seemed inevitable. What he had not expected was that the war should come so soon, and so close to England.

A group of Englishmen stood near the door. From their loud talk he judged them to be supporters of Mosley's British Union of Fascists, typical thugs, all loud talk. They were praising Franco for having the balls to lead an army against Communism. The Germans and Italians, they were saying, also understood the nature of Communism. The world would be a better place if there were more Francos around.

'If Generalissimo Chiang hadn't done the same against the Reds the Communists would be drinking here now and we'd be on a boat home!' one of them said loudly.

Julian could not help feeling that it was fortunate that he was in Wuhan. If he were in Europe he would have no choice: the only reasonable course would be to go to Spain and join the battle. However, it was wretched having to sit here listening to the ravings of people like this.

'The Red Army looted Sichuan, just up the road, during the course of their so-called Long March.'

'Red bastards. They're getting nearer. I'd rather see the Japs here than the Communists!'

Other people in the room had different views. The Germans were too arrogant, harder to control than the Communists. Others insisted that Europeans were at least civilized, and Western countries could reach some sort of agreement. Russians were simply beyond the pale, an inferior race who would not abide by any treaty.

Julian was outraged by the racist sentiments he heard around him, and could not help speaking up: 'It's about time Hitler was assassinated, long overdue, in fact. Force is the only language Nazis understand, not treaties.'

'Go to hell! I don't speak to Reds!'

'Dirty Fascist. What a pity you didn't get a beating in

London.' Julian had indeed once joined a demonstration against the Union of Fascists, but before any fighting began the Fascists had seen they were seriously outnumbered and had beaten a retreat.

Before he knew what was happening he was struck violently in the face, on the nose, and fell back. A second blow followed.

He crouched down under the bar and then aimed a heavy right hook to the man's chin. It hit him square on the jaw and the man fell to the floor, sweeping a row of cups and ashtrays with him. Bits of broken glass sprayed everywhere.

There were alarmed cries from bystanders. Some piled into the fight, others tried to pull them apart.

Julian's assailant pulled himself back upright and was shouting, 'One against one! One against one! Let me handle the Red bastard!'

Julian pushed back those surrounding him. He felt calm and ready for whatever might happen. At Cambridge he had joined a boxing club, although he really was not up to it and was constantly being knocked out by his opponents. But today he was spoiling for a scrap and would give as good as he got. This loudmouth was obviously an East End rough, brought up on street fighting, who relished the fear he could incite in Jews in the street.

By now Julian's nose had started to bleed and the salty taste of blood was in his mouth. He roared and lunged forward but was immediately pulled back. These appeasers infuriated him. After all, the other man had got in the underhand first blow and he was the one who had come off worst.

He shook himself free, but now there were people standing between them. Beside himself with anger, he shouted, 'We either let the Fascists ruin the world or follow the Communists to save it! Nothing in between.'

The White Russian girl rushed over. She tried to persuade him to lie down to stop the bleeding, and went to clean his face.

She wanted to take Julian back to her room for a rest but he pushed her away. He swallowed the remaining blood in his mouth and stormed out of the bar, heading straight back to campus.

On the ferry a fresh river breeze blew on his face and he began to cool down. The Yangtze was wide here, and the boat trip took some time. As the ferry rocked beneath his feet he gazed across to the shore looming darkly ahead, and he remembered how he had first made up his mind to come to China.

When he had applied to the appointments office of Cambridge University for overseas teaching posts, he had put down China without a moment's hesitation. Before leaving Britain he went to see Aunt Virginia and had a long talk with the Woolfs. Leonard, as a political scientist, thought that he had made the right decision and said once again that China was bound to become the centre of a political storm in the coming decades. What happened there would affect the whole world.

Julian was proud of their approval and his determination grew firmer as his ship drew nearer to China. What could be more inspiring than to take part in a revolution? The anti-Fascist stand of the Chinese revolutionaries might give him the opportunity he wanted. The Fascist contagion was spreading, and the complacent response of British intellectuals and the Labour Party back home seemed to him intolerably hollow. Only revolutionaries had the nerve to confront the Fascists head on, and he would not be content until he had also done so.

He had decided to spend some time in a university first, so as to familiarize himself with the situation before making his move. What he had not expected was to fall desperately in love, and be tormented by it to the point of sickness. During all these months, he had refused to be reminded of his original aim, dismissing it as soon as it flashed through his mind. After all, he had plenty of time and a little delay would not matter too much.

He did nothing, cutting himself off from the world around him. Lin had mesmerized him into forgetting that he had come to China in order to alleviate the plight of mankind.

How could he have made sexual pleasure his life's aim, still less love? Lin was only K, number eleven. Women, whether Oriental or European, were all the same: same flesh, same sexual feelings. He had succumbed to Lin's charms, just as he had been enchanted by her splendidly coloured silks, and by the glorious scenery around him. But these were only passing sensations, not a place to rest his spirit for ever.

Nothing will get in my way this time, not even Lin, he vowed. Recalling the ups and downs of their relationship he was prepared to admit he had been cold to her at times. But coldness was better than deception: he could not spend the rest of his life with her. The time she had threatened suicide was when he had most wanted to leave her. That was why he could not bring himself to say things like, 'Please take good care of yourself.' Such touches of tenderness only led to a more painful protraction of the affair.

He wondered briefly how she would go on living without him, but that was not his problem. The whole world would return to the dark ages if they let the Fascists win.

He did not feel this was a betrayal, nor did he have a guilty conscience. He had never promised to be faithful. He had made no oath, nor any clear statement, even when pressurized.

It stops at K, there will be no L or M. The evil confronting the world would not wait for his romances.

Suddenly he felt grateful to the man who had attacked him in the Red House. He had saved him from the misery of this affair, the clinging sentimentalism of his jealousy. A man had to face up to important issues, and act.

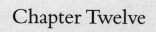

Chapter Twelve

Julian started packing as soon as he reached home. He needed to travel light, but had to take with him a torch, a compass, matches, maps and so on. He would follow the route taken by the Red Army, but until he reached them he should keep quiet about the purpose of his journey.

His Chinese was not good enough for him to embark on such an expedition alone. He needed a guide and interpreter. He thought of Yi, a student in his class who had become a sort of friend.

He had always tried to keep a distance from the students during his affair with Lin. The one exception was Yi, who spoke good English, was intelligent and active in the student movement. But he did not look like an underground Communist – the most publicly visible students generally were not. It did not matter either way. When they arrived at the front line they could separate, there was not much need for language in a war.

While he was packing someone knocked at the bedroom door. It was Vole, reporting that Mrs Dean had called that morning. She said Professor Bell had asked her to have a look at the ceramics and paintings he had bought.

'When did she come?'

'A little past eight.'

Julian's heart skipped a beat. For an instant he felt anguished. She was still in love with him.

But he pulled himself together sternly. He could not let love get in the way of his mission.

He replied that he would send her a note. Vole left after a polite 'good night'. By now it was very late, but he did not feel like sleeping. He had spent the whole day wandering around the city – and he had missed the most important moment, the time when he should have been waiting one last time for his lover. Perhaps it was fate. They had missed each other, and everything now pointed him in a different direction.

He had told the servants that he was going for a trip around the country. There was no need even to ask the department for leave as the strike was now in full swing and there were no more classes. Anyway, the summer vacation would soon be on them. His desertion would hardly be noticed.

Neither was there any need to say goodbye to Lin. He was not going to change his mind.

He was tired of love, which wasn't a bad thing. In any case, it seemed now there was no escape from a full-scale world war. He would not, of course, fight for the British Empire; during the Great War all the men of the Bloomsbury set had refused to participate in the war effort, and registered as conscientious objectors. Patriotic fervour was anathema to them. The war that was now imminent would be different, since it would be fought against Fascists. A war that would eliminate war by spawning an anti-war momentum. There was too much liberalism in his blood for him to fight for King and Country. He would fight, and die, if necessary, not for glory but in defence of his own moral beliefs.

At midnight he called on Yi at the students' dormitory. Yi was of middling height, bespectacled, lively and quick-witted, a typical southern Chinese. He was initially hesitant when he heard Julian's plan. What persuaded him was when Julian told him that they could go as newspaper reporters; he could get them press credentials from the Hankou Reuters office.

Then they discussed the best route. Yi knew that the Red Army had been active in the border area of Sichuan and Shanxi provinces. There had been fierce battles between the Red Army and Sichuan warlords, involving large movements of troops. But recently they seemed to have moved away. There was hardly any news about their exact location. Their best choice was to go and look for clues at their former base area.

They took a boat up the Yangtze, through the Three Gorges, and alighted at Wan Xian. This was a largish town, and Julian tried for a car from the one car-hire company. The proprietor had only three cars, all of them out at that time, although one might come back towards the evening. In fact, an old jeep came back in late afternoon.

Julian paid the deposit and told the driver what route they wanted to take. They bought some dried food and set out the next morning. The bumpy, unpaved road to the north was in a miserable state and the driver complained vociferously. Finally Julian lost patience, and told him to sit behind and let him drive.

'We're lucky there *is* a road,' said Yi. 'We may soon get to an area with no roads at all.'

'If so, we shall hire horses,' Julian returned confidently.

'Money opens all doors,' Yi said with a smile.

Julian and the driver took turns, stopping only when it was too dark to drive safely and they had to find a place to sleep. The further north they went the more miserable and bug-infested the inns became. Eventually they arrived at the north-eastern part of Sichuan Province, where they were told that the main force of the Communist army, which called itself the Fourth Front Army, had left the area only a few months earlier.

It was much more difficult to drive now, the narrow road twisting and turning through the mountains. A single moment of carelessness could send the car rolling over the precipice. After a couple of near misses, Julian decided to give up and dispatch the driver home with the car. Travelling on horseback was far easier, as they would not have to stick to the road but could get from village to village across the mountain passes.

Julian had seen the poverty of the Chinese countryside on his way from Wuhan to Peking. But now, in the late spring of 1936, he was experiencing it at first hand. They passed through Qu County, locally nicknamed 'Porridge County' for the poverty of the people's diet. The local fare, mainly potatoes and yams, was almost indigestible. Whenever they passed a township with a restaurant, even if it was just a shack, they would stop to fill up on noodles and steamed bread. Often they had to resort to buying a meal in a hovel so dirty that nothing but their acute hunger would have persuaded them to eat there. The pair of them carried on heading north-west.

By now they were beginning to see soldiers – whether of the Government or of the local warlords they could not tell. The troops were apparently withdrawing from the battlefields. They were poorly equipped and in tattered uniforms. Discipline seemed lax, and they had clearly been looting as they went. Julian could not help wondering how this raggle-taggle army could withstand a real battle with the well-equipped and well-trained Japanese army.

The horses were tired. They found some fodder and tethered them to a tree, then sat down in the shade for a rest. They began to talk of the academics and writers they knew in Wuhan, who, although recently active in raising funds to support the anti-Japanese war effort, would panic in the face of military defeat, and had no stomach for battle. Who then in this China could stop the Japanese advance?

Now they had entered the mountainous regions of the border area of Sichuan. This kind of place, Yi said, was usually infested with bandits in peacetime. It looked as though there had been recent fighting here. The population was sparse; the villages had suffered heavy damage. For miles there was not even a house left standing. From time to time they saw corpses, although they could not make out whether they were soldiers or civilians, or on which side. The bodies had become unrecognizable, mere blackened heaps, partially dismembered, possibly by wild animals. The two men rode by, trying not to look too closely.

All of a sudden Julian pulled his horse up short, stifling a cry of horror. There, hanging from a pine tree on the edge of a cliff, was the naked body of a man. Stuck in its chest bone was a chopping knife. The stench of decomposing flesh filled the air. Julian covered his nose with one hand and urged his terrified horse into a gallop.

They rode as fast as they could towards human habitation and away from this evidence of atrocities. Now they heard sporadic gunfire, some quite near. They did not know who was shooting whom, soldiers or bandits, or hunters. After all, with the land untilled what were the surviving local people supposed to live on? The horror of what they had seen lingered in Julian's mind, and he feared there was worse to come.

To relieve his tension he began to talk to Yi about women. He had never discussed this topic with a Chinese student, and had only a vague notion of their ideas about sex. They were obviously not as sexually active as their Western counterparts. But right now, as they made their way through this unreal landscape, talking about women seemed a good way of distracting themselves.

Being the favoured son of a rich southern family, Yi was comparatively experienced in these matters and seemed willing to talk; he was far from being a prude. Julian thought he might be able to shed some light on the Daoist Art of Love, and asked him if he knew anything of it.

Yi's response was immediate: the Art was, he said, nothing but feudal superstition, and the most corrupt, backward-looking and immoral part of Chinese culture.

Julian was taken aback by such uncompromising con-demnation, but gathered that it was what most people in Chinese intellectual circles believed. Yi had heard of some Western Sinologists translating the Chinese erotic novels, *The Golden Lotus* and *Flesh Prayer Mat*. He found this insulting to Chinese culture. Chinese students in Germany had even stoned the house of the German translator in protest, breaking all its windows.

Julian recalled his own reading of *The Golden Lotus* and was a little upset by his companion's censoriousness.

'Have you read anything on the Daoist Art of Love?' he asked.

Yi shook his head and added that frankly he would not read about it even if he were given the chance. An evil landlord in Hunan who collected and printed these books had been executed by the Communists in 1927. In Yi's view that was one of their more commendable actions.

Julian shuddered at the thought of Yi, this sophisticated young man, praising this kind of violent moralism, and changed the subject. He started to talk about what was considered beautiful in European women, and asked Yi about the criteria for beauty in Chinese women. Yi answered by asking Julian in his turn what he found beautiful about Chinese women.

'How their bodies smell,' Julian responded rather vaguely.

Yi smiled. 'Chinese women certainly have less body odour than foreigners. In fact, body odour is called "barbarian smell" in Chinese.'

'I was thinking about body fragrance.'

'I don't know about that.'

Julian was unwilling to let it go at that and pursued his line of questioning.

'What about women who have no pubic hair or armpit hair?'

Yi laughed in embarrassment and said that he had only heard stories and had no personal experience of such a woman.

'What stories?'

'Well, women like that are supposed to be White Tiger Stars, who descend to the human world and are likely to cause the death of their husbands.'

This was a surprise to Julian. 'But that's just superstition!' he protested.

'Superstition or no, just don't go to bed with a woman like that, whatever the circumstances.'

'But how would one know? I mean, Chinese couples are not allowed to get to know each before marriage, let alone have pre-marital sex!'

'The matchmakers are responsible for providing clients with such essential information. Matchmaking used to be serious business in China, and lucrative, too. Also, the husband's family could send the woman back home, so long as the marriage had not been consummated.'

'Then who could those women find to marry them?' Julian asked anxiously.

'Only someone who could not afford a better wife,' said Yi. 'And, of course, more educated men who don't go in for superstitions. But in ordinary Chinese society these women can't even go into prostitution. I heard the story of a man who went to a prostitute with no pubic hair and didn't notice it until after he had had sex. He smashed up the brothel, to rid himself of bad luck.'

'Didn't you say it was bad news only for her husband?'

'That's a Chinese euphemism. Any man who has sex with such a woman is bound to come to a bad end.'

It occurred to Julian that it was Cheng's turn first, then his. And he smiled wryly to himself.

This was the very opposite of Lin's explanation that, according to the Art, lack of pubic hair was a refinement bred into certain women. He would rather believe her. But he felt sorry for her. Women with such a beautiful and sensuous physical trait should not be subjected to contempt and discriminated against. Whichever was true, he was beginning to learn that there might be a price to pay in China both for fighting against Fascism and for enjoying sexual freedom.

The flat surface of the rock beside the road was marked with illegible writing. New slogans were scrawled over old ones and the rock was covered with layers of different colours. The road was high up on the hill, and the slogans were visible from a considerable distance. They passed through a village and were told that there were no men left in it, only old women and little girls. The men in their families had either been killed by the White Army as Red Army supporters or by the Red Army as White Army supporters. Those still alive had either joined the Red Army or been conscripted by the White Army.

They heard the sound of fast-flowing water. From the crest of a hill they saw a large expanse of green forest and a fast-flowing river below them. The pebbled foreshore was wide and clean, and a village was just visible in the distance. They dismounted and tried to find the locality on the map.

'This must be Zitong County,' Yi said.

The water was so clear that they threw down their knapsacks and waded in up to their waists, leading the horses. It was deliciously cool. Only now did Julian realize how filthy he had become during their hot days of travelling. They had tried to keep themselves clean by washing whenever there was water available, but nothing was as clean as this. He picked a few pebbles with brilliant mineral streaks as a souvenir and put them in his trouser pocket.

Picking up their bags, they led the horses back up the slope. Suddenly they saw a row of rifle-barrels with bayonets pointing at them. The soldiers shouted something.

Julian did not need a translation to understand the order and raised his hands obediently. He signalled to Yi, who shouted to them that Julian was a foreign reporter. The squad leader called him over. Yi took out their credentials and launched into an explanation, pointing at Julian.

Then the soldiers lowered their rifles. Yi came back to say that these were the Sichuan warlord troops. This was a war zone, they had told him, and nobody was allowed to wander around freely.

They would have to go and see the officer in charge of the administration of the county. 'Luckily, you have a big nose,' Yi chuckled. 'At such times foreigners arouse less suspicion than Chinese.'

They were led to a nearby checkpoint manned by the patrol. After a lengthy wait, a mounted staff officer came to escort them to the headquarters of the brigade.

Yi said, 'This used to be a Red area. It looks like this is the end of our journey. The Red Army has moved west.'

What does he mean, 'end of our journey'? thought Julian. It was only the starting point. At least they had a lead now. If Yi didn't want to go on for whatever reason, he would find a local guide and follow the Red Army westwards.

The town was not very different from those they had seen previously. Perhaps because the army had its headquarters here, there were more people in the streets, and the place was bustling. It even boasted an ancient gate and a short stretch of city wall. Some of the old two-storey wooden houses, though dark with age, still stood. Others had been reduced by the war to heaps of charcoal and blackened bricks.

The streets were paved in limestone. Towards them came an ox-cart, its load covered with torn matting. The stench as it passed was indescribable. It was followed by a large group of cheerful children, the smallest of whom were not just ragged but actually bare-bottomed. As they pressed themselves back to let the cart pass they were appalled to see protruding from under the mat the clawlike hands and feet of human bodies.

It was clear that there had been fierce fighting in the area not long before. Yet somehow Julian did not think that these corpses had been gathered from a battlefield.

They were brought to the army headquarters. The brigade commander was an angry-faced man wearing neither army cap nor uniform jacket. At the sight of the British correspondent and his translator he put on a welcoming smile and invited them into the house. His soldiers were sent to feed their horses. The house, with its attractive lacquered furniture, was grand in comparison with the other houses in the town. Julian thought that it must belong to some local landlord.

'I assume that your news bulletins will faithfully record the achievements of our brigade in pacifying the area.' He was clearly making an effort to impress, and used the most flowery language he could muster.

Julian told him that his duty as a correspondent was to give an objective report. He hoped that the commander would provide him with assistance and permit him to go to the front and carry out his investigations there.

The commander sat down, puffing on his cigarette, and shook his head. He said the war was over in this area. The Red Army had been annihilated and a total victory won. But the area once occupied by Communist gangsters was by no means secure – routed Red Army elements were still carrying out murders. For their own safety he could neither allow them to stay here nor to go further on.

They argued back and forth for some time. In the end the commander consented to allow them to interview some POWs to acquire some material for their reports.

He then called one of his adjutants and told him to escort them to the prison. Julian also noticed that he added a few words in a low tone in the man's ear.

The few better houses in the town had all been taken over by troops. In the fields there were only a few trees and a small amount of sorghum, while weeds grew waist high. It was two or three in the afternoon and very hot. The stench of decomposing bodies filled the air. In the distant fields wisps of smoke could be seen, presumably from people cooking the few pieces of food they could find.

They were led across a bridge suspended over a creek and into a heavily guarded fortress. They went across a courtyard and down into a dimly lit cellar, furnished with a few stools and a table. The stone walls were stained with smoke, and by other unidentifiable substances. There was a rather sinister smell of mould mixed with something far worse. The adjutant asked them to sit down and lit a kerosene lamp, which brightened the room considerably.

They were told that this was the jail and this cellar the interrogation room. The prisoners were led in one by one. They were all young and dressed in tattered rags. Some were wounded, and all were weighed down by heavy wooden cangues. A soldier cradling a gun stood on guard by the door. The prisoners were all in peasants' clothes, and most were barefoot. It was hard to tell whether they were villagers or soldiers. According to the adjutant they were all Red Army soldiers captured when the Red Army was defeated.

In a Chinese civil war prisoners were traditionally pressed into service as conscripts for the victorious army. However, they were told that these young men had been members of the Communist local government and involved in the murder of fellow villagers. Yi said their dialect was difficult to understand, particularly because they were nervous and talked fast. He had to stop them from time to time in order to keep up with his translation for Julian.

Each of the stories was very similar to the one that preceded it: they were peasant boys from the nearby villages. When the Communists came they were mobilized into staging an 'agrarian uprising', during which all the male members of the landlord's family were killed, and their land, cattle, houses, wives and daughters redistributed. The result had split the village into two irreconcilable camps. If there was one member of the family who had taken part in the killing, the rest of the family had no choice but to join the supporters of the Red Army. And the relatives of the murdered had no choice but to join the supporters of the White Army.

'Did you murder anyone?'

They all shook their heads tearfully and begged them to believe that they had been falsely accused: it was a case of mistaken identity, they had had nothing to do with it. Obviously they took the interview as another interrogation.

Julian was a little disappointed. There was not much he could learn. He would have liked to end it, when another prisoner was escorted in, one even younger, perhaps fourteen or fifteen, wearing only ragged short pants. He was malnourished and pitifully thin, and his ribs stuck out. He walked in with his head held high and declared proudly that he had indeed chopped off the head of his landlord's son. The local Communist Party representative had encouraged the peasants to rise in rebellion, and asked if he had the courage to take the lead. He had courage enough for anything. After their raid on the landlord's house he was given the job of beheading the landlord's son, who was the same age as he. The first hack was not sufficient to finish the job. The young master had screamed like a pig at the slaughter. The commissar urged him to strike again.

'Why did you kill him?'

'To be Red is to chop off heads, of course,' the youngster replied. 'After a few goes his head was still connected to his neck but he did not scream any more. It just hung down on his chest and did not roll onto the ground.'

The youngster said these words with obvious regret, looking at his skinny arms weighed down by the heavy cangue.

Julian could bear it no more. As vomit rose in his throat he stumbled out of the interrogation room, pushing past the guard, and ran up the stairs. The bright sunshine in the courtyard almost blinded him. Squatting on the ground, he retched again and again.

Yi came up behind him. 'Are you all right?'

Julian did not want to look weaker than Yi. Without replying he got up and went back in as if nothing had happened. But he went into the wrong room — an empty room filled with instruments of punishment and torture, some still stained with blood. They must have stored these things here when tidying up the interrogation room for them. Flies were buzzing around. He felt sick again and returned to the courtyard. He was unwilling to go into any other room for fear of what he might see.

Yi said to the officer, 'It's hot. The weather is too hot for him.'

The soldiers led them back to headquarters. The commander was no longer there but he had ordered his staff to prepare them a decent meal and get them a room at the local inn.

The dinner was adequate, there was meat in it but neither of them had any appetite. After that they were led to the inn, which seemed to have been deserted for a long time. It was a two-storey wooden house, very dark. The proprietor was an old woman, who was terrified at the sight of a 'foreign devil' and afraid to mention even one word about how much they had to pay.

There were two beds in the room but no bedding. The adjutant got the soldiers to bring two new military bedding packs. The summer night was hot, but they still had to cover themselves up in order to protect themselves from being dive-bombed by mosquitoes. 'We're lucky,' Yi muttered to Julian. 'It's your foreign face that's keeping us from being harassed by gangsters or soldiers.'

The inn was on the main market street. The wooden window was open. The only noises were the footsteps of patrolling soldiers and the sound of crickets in the corner. The old woman crept quietly in to snuff out the wavering flame of the lamp.

The room was pitch dark. Only a square patch of night sky showed through the window.

Yi tossed and turned on his bed. Julian lay there silent. He felt his earlier behaviour had been unworthy of him. A war was a war, and a revolution was a revolution. There were no nice ways to kill people.

All he had wanted on their trip from Wuhan was to find the Red Army on its Long March and join the Chinese Revolution. Now he had seen just a very little bit of revolutionary action, and his body had revolted against it. It was a terrible humiliation.

There was some air now in the room; it was cooler and more comfortable. But he felt on the verge of another defeat. What was he to do now?

Early the next morning they were woken by the sound of drumbeats. It was noisy in the street. Soldiers were standing with bayoneted rifles on both sides, keeping the disorderly crowd at bay. Julian was surprised that in a place like this, devastated by war, there were still so many people. It was like a fair-day, with throngs of people from the nearby villages milling around.

They stood at the window, and since their room was on the second floor they had a good view of what was happening on the street. Three ox-carts rolled slowly by, each carrying about twenty people, all in heavy cangues, some of whom they had seen yesterday. At the side of each cart walked expressionless executioners, carrying gleaming broad swords. Some of the onlookers were weeping, some were shouting imprecations, but most watched in silence.

The street was not long; the procession turned round at the end and returned to the spot, just opposite their inn, that was to be used as the execution ground. The soldiers forced the prisoners down from the ox-cart one by one. An officer holding a sheet of paper read out their details in a heavy Sichuan accent. Each 'Red criminal' was identified along with his crime, and it was declared in all solemnity that the death sentence was to be carried out as an example to others and so on and so forth.

The criminals, now kneeling on the ground, were pale and shivering. The soldiers removed the cangues and tied their hands behind their backs. Then the executioner's assistant pulled roughly at the head of each one to expose the neck, and the executioner raised high his sword. Yells, cheers and wails rose from the crowds.

'Close the window,' Yi was saying loudly from where he sat on the bed. 'Please close the window.'

Julian had long since backed away from the window, but seeing that Yi was in a worse state than he was he had to go and do it. This was easier said than done. The wooden frame was old and warped and he almost broke the glass when he tried to close it.

He heard a feeble voice shouting, 'Long live the Red Army! Long live Revolution!' It was the boy – the only one who had acknowledged his part in the killings. Julian involuntarily looked down and saw the ground drenched with blood still draining from bodies without heads. He closed his eyes as the voice came again, 'Revolution —' before it was cut off with a swishing sound. Julian leaped back from the window as if to avoid the gush of blood. He collapsed onto the floor.

'Oh,' he groaned. He felt as if his lungs were on fire and he could hardly breathe. 'Why? Why do they need to be so cruel? Revolutionaries, counter-revolutionaries… Why so cruel?'

The old woman stood in the doorway to their room, dazed, without even acknowledging their presence. They sat without speaking or moving.

'No,' Julian thought. 'This kind of revolution is not for me. There's too much stirring up of class hatred, too much murder. The Chinese peasants are poor, so are the workers, but they have not reached the stage of revolution yet. Even if they do want a revolution, why should it be so bloody, so riddled with hatred?'

He thought of the cyanide he had brought with him. His ideas about the revolution had been far too naive. He felt capable of putting an end to himself, but he could never have acted like the commissar who handed the boy a knife and urged him to go on hacking at the neck of another boy.

What role could he play in this struggle? The noise outside the window was still going on, yet Julian no longer felt a part of it: his dreams of joining in had been shattered for ever on this early morning in this mountain town.

When they rode out there were twenty or so new heads hanging on the town gate, dripping blood. Julian was in no mood to look. They rode back the way they had come, crossing the shallow river and the green forest, anxious to put the greatest distance possible between themselves and this awful place.

It was noon when they arrived at another county town. They were told there had been an accident on the mountain road and several horses and men had fallen together into the gully. They would have to take a different route eastwards. He consoled himself as he rode that he was not a deserter. What they were fighting for was not European-style socialism or liberalism. Atrocities were normal in revolutions in this part of the world, but he was not Asian and he did not have to be dragged into it. Even where the cause was just there was still a difference between East and West. The gap between them was too wide for him to bridge.

They waited for a meal in a modest, quiet restaurant, and Julian found in his backpack the yellow handkerchief with its bamboo pattern. The soft material clung to his fingers, reminding him of the way their bodies had clung together. He looked closely at the embroidered initial. Suddenly he recalled reading in a sixth-century Jewish scripture from Syria or Palestine that K was the letter of life.

As they made their way south to the Yangtze the image of Lin came back to him more and more clearly, rousing him from his depression. Once more he found himself under her spell, longing, in the stillness of the night, to hear her voice, see her smile.

Yes, she was the person who should share his future. If only they could live together permanently, wherever it was. Just as she once said, she was part of his life. He would prove to her that he was not as selfish as she imagined. He had always loved her, albeit in his own fashion, but he could also love her in the manner that she desired.

Once the idea was firmly established in his mind he realized that he had always felt this way. He had just needed some time to clear his head. Now Lin would bring him back from the battlefield.

He thought how unusual she was within her own culture. Cheng might consider himself a man educated enough to rise above the popular superstitions like the White Tiger Stars stories and accept Lin for his wife. But precisely because of that same rationalism, Cheng could reject the whole set of Daoist theories and sexual practices in which she genuinely believed. Lin could not flourish in such an atmosphere of sexual repression. What kind of a marriage was that for her?

He understood why she had come to depend on him. She was sandwiched between the different tiers of her culture. Neither the progressive nor traditional elements could accept her entirely: she was effectively an outcast in her own country. On the other hand, he, as a foreigner, could stand aloof from both. He did not have to believe popular superstition or accept the 'progressiveness' of modern China. He could believe whatever made him happy and treat the rest pragmatically.

Theirs was an unusual relationship – but that fitted with the rest of his life. His own mother had a totally unconventional love life. She took a bisexual man as her lifelong companion, something that no one in society could understand.

On that summer day, in the desolate countryside of Sichuan, Julian suddenly awoke as if from a dream and discovered that the only thing really precious to him in China was what he already had. When Lin invited him to Peking for that unforgettable winter holiday it was so that she could share with him everything previously denied to her: her pent-up desires and long-suppressed ability to love unreservedly. When she laid bare her beautiful body she was holding nothing back, she was showing him her whole spiritual world.

It had taken him a long time to get back to the Great River; and to what was waiting patiently for him on the other side.

In another two years he would be thirty, and into his middle years. The men in his family matured slowly. He should have a good future. They would have children. It would not matter where they lived, so long as it was far from turmoil and hatred, in a place where they could devote themselves to poetry.

The most important thing was to get back to her as soon as possible. The earlier the better. Sitting waiting for his dinner in the little restaurant, he was impatient. Yi went away to relieve himself and did not return for a while. They polished off the bean porridge, the fried dumplings and the fried pepper with shredded potato. Then he said to Yi that they should hurry back to Wuhan as quickly as possible.

They rode on, bathed in brilliant sunlight, leaving the tiny restaurant behind them.

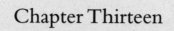

Chapter Thirteen

It was five o'clock on a late summer afternoon when Julian climbed Luojia Hill again. The flowers that had carpeted the hill when he left were beginning to die back. The leaves were turning from green to yellow and orange. Looking down from his vantage point at the three cities of Wuhan, Julian felt he had finally grown up. Somehow he was as old as Lin now. When he arrived at the junction in the path, he thought for a while about whether to go to Lin's house first.

He had gone off without any warning, had disappeared without trace. What would she think of him now? His longing to see her turned to dread. He began to fear that she might have cooled towards him or even forgotten him. It would be a test of her love, of whether she loved him as fervently as he loved her.

As if in answer to his question a rainbow gradually emerged in the sky.

It was a good sign.

He looked down at East Lake. The sky above and the waters below were beginning to acquire the almost garish colours of evening.

The servants were taken aback by Julian's unexpected return. Why had he not sent a telegram so that they could have gone to Hankou to meet him? They started to busy themselves with preparing food. Julian's priority, however, was a good bath. After the boat trip down the Yangtze and the ferry he was filthy from head to foot. His hair, long neglected, had turned into an unruly mess of curls, and a beard covered his cheeks and chin. He must look rather like a barbarian in an ancient Chinese painting.

After a bath and a shave he changed into clean clothes. When he went downstairs the servants said that supper would be ready in minutes. He was ravenous but decided his meal could wait. Even though it meant arriving at Lin's house with fallen leaves stuck to his shoes, he slipped and slithered down the path through the woods as fast as he could.

Julian said he wanted to see the dean. The servant went in and returned to say that Professor Cheng would see him in the study upstairs. That was unusual, but then he saw that they had guests in the drawing room and in the garden. Julian went straight on up. It was only the second time he had been upstairs in their house. Cheng was sitting behind the desk, with Lin standing at his shoulder. Cheng got up to shake hands with him, but Lin remained motionless. Julian presented his apologies for taking absence without leave.

Cheng received him graciously and, far from admonishing him, seemed glad to see him back. The strike had actually been over before the end of last term, since the students needed grades to graduate. After the summer vacation the new academic year had just begun. They could not find Julian so they had found a temporary teacher. Now that Julian was back, they would dismiss the substitute. 'The only thing we knew was that your servants told us you were travelling around the country. But no one knew how to find you.' Now he hoped that Julian could continue with his very productive teaching till the end of his two-year contract.

While he was talking the servant brought in tea.

Julian understood that Cheng was indicating that they would not renew the contract with him when his two years expired. But he did not care about that. His eyes had moved to Lin. She was very simply dressed, with none of the striking glamour he had known before. But that was just how he wanted to see her, just like an ordinary wife. She was standing behind Cheng's chair, and it was as much as he could do to take his eyes off her and pay attention to what Cheng was saying.

She had her back to the light and it was difficult for him to make out her expression, but he could see that her face was thinner. When their eyes met again he was filled with remorse. She evaded his gaze, as if not wanting him to notice anything unusual. But he could not help seeing her tears. Yes, tears, so that she had to take off her glasses to wipe her eyes.

She still loves me! Lin wiped the glasses with a handkerchief and held them in her hands. On her right wrist was a red silk ribbon.

Unable to think of anything else to say he stood up to say goodbye. Cheng also stood up, and accompanied him to the door. Lin followed behind. Away from the window he could see her more clearly. There was no mistaking the desperation on her face.

Lin disappeared downstairs into the kitchen to oversee the preparations for dinner. Cheng invited him to join them and their guests. But Julian had not had a chance to exchange a word with Lin before she vanished. No chance to explain anything. He could see that he would not have the opportunity even if he stayed. So he politely declined dinner, and the brandy that Cheng tried to press on him, and took his leave.

It was a rainy night. The beating of the raindrops on the window-panes lulled Julian into a peaceful mood. His mind was made up. The sound of the rain took him back to his mother's garden on a wet afternoon. In his mind he was travelling home, greeting his delighted mother. They would be together again. The evening air was pleasantly fresh. He took another bath, opened the windows a little and fell into a peaceful sleep.

He was awakened the next morning by a naked, soft body, fragrantly musky, pressing against his. He did not need to open his eyes to know who it was. It felt truly wonderful to hold her again in his arms, just as he had imagined and dreamed. Her tongue, her hair, her skin; he was afraid to open his eyes in case he was dreaming.

Then she reached for him and pulled him towards her, away from his mad adventure.

Their lovemaking was gentle, without the kind of desperate need of long-separated lovers, like a married couple's familiar intimacy. They started to move rhythmically, relishing the joy of their bodies' close contact. They lavished caresses on each other – on face, hair, neck, shoulder and breast, every part that had been untouched for so long.

They were no longer just illicit lovers, whether they admitted it openly or not. Their ease with each other's bodies, the way they moved together, was proof enough. They had made love so many times, and now for the first time he felt that the only thing that could give him real happiness was a wife whom he deeply loved.

Lin did not ask him why he had gone away without saying goodbye, or even where he had been. In fact, she made no reproaches at all, just gave sighs of pleasure as she clung tight and lavished kisses on him.

He felt as though he did not know precisely how long they had been away from each other. It felt like a long time, and they had narrowly escaped being parted for ever.

Thank God, he thought, for bringing us back together. Now, finally, he opened his eyes to look at the woman he loved so much.

On her right wrist was the thin red ribbon that he had seen yesterday. He asked about it. She said that it was to exorcize evil, and would work for the man she loved as well. It was the first time he had heard her voice for a very long time. She really was here, it was not a dream.

This time as he thrust into her he discovered a very simple rule: when they looked into each other's eyes his orgasm almost overwhelmed him, but when they kissed each other gently with closed eyes the feeling gradually ebbed. So Julian did not ejaculate, even though he had not touched a woman for such a long time. No physical rush knocked him out of control, nor pushed him to the usual tautness that almost made him burst. For the first time he had the astonishing sensation of enjoying repeated orgasms.

Was this the secret of the Art of Love? It took practice, but more importantly a power of feeling that went beyond simple arousal. It required genuine love. For now he understood that when you loved someone deeply enough you naturally wanted to give her the greatest possible enjoyment. Your mind focused on self-control and this allowed you to prolong your own pleasure, too.

The bed seemed to have expanded to fill the universe, to be actually moving in space. He caught a glimpse of the light blue of her cheongsam where it lay on the floor. The reddish-purple blooms on the fabric, as fresh and fragrant as their love, swam before his eyes. Time was no longer important.

A series of tremendous bangs shook the door downstairs. Neither of them reacted to the noise. They lay there holding each other, and the sounds seemed to him like a careless oarsman on the lake at night, allowing the oar to bang the side of the boat. But the knocking continued, loud and angry.

They heard the servants hurrying to the door. Only now did he remember that he had not sent them out and told them to stay away till nine o'clock. It must be long past nine. Neither of them panicked. In fact, they felt resentment at being disturbed, and refused to withdraw from the other's body.

Wizard came up to knock lightly at the bedroom door and said, 'It's Dean Cheng. He wants to see Professor Bell this minute.'

In his arms Lin gave an involuntary quiver. They had feared this moment for so long and now it had come. Julian jumped out of bed and threw on his clothes. He was just buttoning his shirt up when the door was pushed open. They had even forgotten to bolt it. In came Cheng.

Cheng stood there, pale with anger. He was an imposing figure in his gown, and not as gaunt as Julian remembered him. He pointed a finger at Julian and appeared to struggle to put his fury into words.

'You are not a gentleman!' he finally accused, his voice full of indignation.

Julian had been wondering what he would say and had no idea how he might reply in his turn. Cheng's wording, however, actually made him laugh.

'Well, I have never wanted to be a gentleman. There certainly aren't any among my family and friends.'

Cheng did not seem to be listening. Instead, he said again, 'You do not behave like a gentleman.'

With that he stopped. It was as if he was in such a paroxysm of rage that words would not come. This thought had the effect of arousing Julian's pity. After all, nothing in Cheng's English education could have prepared him for such a moment. He did not even understand words in the same way Julian did. His English had been learned from books. It had no subtlety or force of expression.

So Julian continued to sit behind the desk, and waited to see what Cheng would say or do next. But Cheng fell irritatingly silent and appeared to be concentrating his efforts on looking anywhere except at the bed.

Julian turned round and was stunned to see Lin in bed, naked as before and wrapped only in the bed sheet. Her dress and a pair of shoes lay on the floor. There was nothing else. She had run to him as before with just a dress over her naked body, and since the mornings were no longer chill he had not noticed.

He began to feel disorientated. How had they arrived at this moment? It occurred to him that this time she had stayed longer than usual. She had not brought her watch, nor had they checked the time. He had no idea what time she had come. Perhaps the servants had seen her when she came in. How strange that she had not carefully bolted the door as she did normally.

A horrible suspicion flashed into his mind. Could she possibly have set him up? Could she have led her husband here so that he would catch them red-handed in bed together? But what for?

Perhaps it was a last-ditch attempt to force his hand. If she created a crisis, there would be a showdown – after which she would have to divorce Cheng, and he would be forced to marry her. She would no longer be the prisoner of Julian's ceaseless wavering.

It was not impossible that Lin's love had turned to a desire for revenge. He cursed himself for not having made the time to talk to her, as he had planned. He had only wanted to tell her that he was prepared to commit himself to their relationship, that they could stay together always. How happy he would have made her!

Their lovemaking today had gone on so long that they had never given themselves a chance to talk. During his absence she must have been making up her mind too. She must have decided on a desperate plan, and today was the day she had put it into execution – she was never afraid of action once she had made her mind up.

Why had she not waited another day? Another half an hour? Why had she given him no hint of what she was proposing to do, instead of forcing all three of them into this corner, from which there was no escape.

Yes, he was trapped. He was faced with the thing he most feared: losing his freedom of choice. Surely she knew him well enough to know that there was no way he would allow himself to be coerced into this kind of a decision. What a dangerous creature this Chinese woman was.

He gave an involuntary shudder, which brought him to his senses. It was much more likely that Cheng had known about their affair for a long time; perhaps he and Lin had already quarrelled but had kept it quiet. Cheng would have hoped that

Lin would eventually return to her senses. In this way he could save their marriage and their reputation, on the campus and in Chinese literary circles. This was why he had decided to turn a blind eye. Certainly he had never been anything other than politeness itself with Julian.

However, something must have happened while he was absent. Something that caused Cheng to feel he could not afford to let things drag on. Possibly Lin did something foolish – from her pallor and the look of desperation he had seen on her face yesterday he suspected she might have put into action her threat of suicide. Perhaps she had even felt remorse on being saved, and had promised to put an end to her affair with him.

He recalled that during their lovemaking Lin had murmured, as if to herself, 'You went away, why come back now?'

It was also possible that his servants had long ago betrayed him to the dean. From the first day he came to the house he had disliked the idea of having them live with him. He had known instinctively that they would spy on him. It would have been so easy for Cheng to find out – in fact it would not have been a surprise to discover that he had known about it from the very beginning. In which case he had to acknowledge that Cheng had been very forbearing with his wife.

If Cheng had decided to take action today, it must have been carefully considered.

E. M. Forster, another father figure in his life, had once told his mother that in spite of his wild behaviour Julian was a traditional English gentleman to the core. As he stood here now, Julian finally understood what Forster had meant. The fanatical love of this Chinese woman, like the violence of the Revolution and everything else Chinese, was simply too alien for him to comprehend or accept.

He looked at Lin sitting in bed. She did not meet his gaze; there was a seemingly abstracted, almost mad expression on her face, as if she knew that what she waited for would never come.

He saw Cheng raise his shaking finger again, ready to repeat his accusations of ungentlemanly behaviour. And he knew what he must do.

He stood up calmly and said to Cheng, 'I can only offer you my most profound apologies. I take total responsibility for everything. In fact, I wish to tender my resignation here and now and shall leave China as soon as I possibly can.'

He walked out of the bedroom and started downstairs. Lin had been completely silent up till that moment, but now he heard a wild cry from the room behind him. She was probably cursing him; he did not understand the words. But there was no mistaking her anguish and desperation.

He expected to hear her crying at any moment. He stood for a few seconds on the stairs, but heard nothing.

The journey home involved changing ships in Hong Kong, and he was forced to put up in a hotel for a short time. He was desperately homesick. To help ward off his longing to return to China, a longing which often overwhelmed him and always when he least expected it, he wrote to his mother and made the novel suggestion that they should build a swimming pool in the garden. A little water could not match up to the vast East Lake or the Yangtze, but it might still serve to console him.

Wuhan was not only far away from home on the map. His months there also seemed to have lasted a lifetime. Mother must have had almost a hundred letters from him. Yet however intense his experiences in China, it had only actually been a tiny part of his life. He felt certain that he would never again love and be loved. The conviction filled him with remorse, but was not actually painful.

In the streets of Hong Kong he tried his best to avoid looking at women who bore any resemblance to her. He never wanted to see her again. In the middle of the night, however, he awoke soaked in sweat. She had appeared to him in a dream, dressed completely in black, a colour he had never seen her wear.

Lin would not let him hear her cry, not in his house nor in his dream. She preserved that last shred of self-respect. She had the right to love him. She refused to be treated unfairly, to be loved only secretively. She refused to let him treat her as unequal.

On that fateful morning when they had been discovered together she had seen right through him. She knew that he was no less racist that any of the other Westerners in China. The only difference was that he was unwilling to recognize it. He still had a deep-seated contempt for the Chinese, even for the one he loved so madly. His decision that morning to cut himself off from her in that way was typical of his European arrogance.

It was painful for him to acknowledge all this. He had thought himself a good internationalist, but had treated China as if it were an exotic distraction. Now there was no way for him to turn except to the West, to find love or war.

The boat sailed out of the bay and veered slowly westwards, into the vastness of the ocean. When the huge continent was no more than an indistinct line on the horizon his pain gradually began to dull. Now the ship was just a dot between the boundless water and the empty sky. His sorrow was no longer bitter: it had become a sort of soft melancholy, which he was learning to accept as part of himself. He stood on the deck and watched the sea and sky turn gradually transparent, and the transparency glow with an ethereal light.

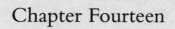

Chapter Fourteen

On July 7th, 1937 the Japanese army attacked Peking, launching a full-scale war against China. The decisive battle of the Spanish Civil War, the battle of Brunete, began at about the same time.

A month earlier Lin had heard from the British woman in the department that Julian had gone to Spain to fight in the Spanish Civil War. She took out all the letters she had written to him after he left Wuhan. She had meant to send them to him in England but had not done so. Now there was no need. She arranged them methodically, according to the date of writing, tied each month in a separate bundle and put them away.

It was unusually hot in Wuhan, with the temperature rising higher every day. No doubt it was the same in Spain. Lin often went to Julian's old house, his key in her hand, as if he were still living there.

She had stopped writing, apart from the letters, bound together with thin cord, and sank into a gradually deepening silence, refusing to communicate with her husband or indeed with anyone else. When it rained she would sit at the window cross-legged, as the hours succeeded one another until nightfall. She gazed impassively at the dense foliage of the garden beyond which nothing was visible. It was as if she were in a state of suspended animation. No emotions – not loneliness, not despair – touched her. She dressed only in black and white. Her coloured clothes had been put away in a trunk. She did not add mothballs to them, since she would not need them any more.

The fires of war blazed from north to south, and Wuhan had become a centre of mobilization. The Chinese rose against the invaders, and the campus of Wuhan University was furiously busy. But the war, like the rest of life, passed Lin by.

One day as she was pacing her room, her eyes shining, she looked into her mirror and saw a woman more beautiful than ever. There was no doubt in her mind that Julian would meet his death in Spain. She knew him so well – he had a death-wish just as she did. The only difference was that he had wanted to be killed by others, while she had the courage to kill herself.

It was mid-July, the time of the Festival of the Dead. The netherworld opened its gate wide to welcome all comers.

In a white gown, she sat in the centre of the floor. In front of her was a circle of candles. During the festival people burned paper money, and paper furniture, too, to provide for their deceased relatives. She closed her eyes and saw shadowy images holding aloft paper houses, paper dresses, paper ox-carts, carriages and sedans ascending Luojia Hill from the Yangtze far below.

In front of her was a bronze vessel from which rose curls of smoke. The bundles of letters were now no more than a heap of ashes. It was the best way to ensure Julian would receive them all.

Towards sunset, those downstairs in the house heard the heavy thud of a falling body. There was a frantic running up and down stairs, lights were switched on, doors banged open and shut. It was not the first time that Lin had tried to kill herself. After several such attempts, Professor Cheng and his servants were accustomed to reacting instantly.

At the hospital, already full to bursting with war wounded, harassed doctors left her on a wheeled stretcher in the corridor to await treatment. In the dim light Cheng sat motionless beside her, no emotion visible on his face.

Lin lay unable to speak, but semi-conscious. She had done this before, because it had been the only way to bring Julian back to her. Once she resorted to this method he had to come back, just as he had returned a year earlier, after he had disappeared.

Yes, he was coming towards her, as she had known he would be, from the end of the corridor where the morgue was, smiling in his customary ironic way. He was wearing army uniform, with boots and helmet.

She closed her eyes in joy. He was beside her. Her clothes fell from her, and her nipples hardened and ached at the touch of his cold fingers. She raised her arms to embrace him, and her lips parted to meet his kiss. Julian embraced her tightly and entered her. Their bodies were bathed in sweat, glued together. They were locked in the climax of their mutual love, yin and yang revolving one around the other, the glittering Great River surging about them.

'That's strange,' a nurse was saying, 'I only hung this white cloth curtain a few minutes ago. How can there be blood stains on it already?'

Lin didn't hear her. But she knew that the Festival of the Dead was not over yet.

Lin's poems to Julian

Beijing

Our self-portraits

Can't you see what I see
in this twig foaming with plum flowers?
A whole quarry-load of granite eyes
have cracked, waiting for it to blossom –
but now the explosion is finally happening,
as your words light the fuse to my heart:
'Till old, we sleep.'

I look away to a winter vase-landscape,
thinking: that's where I lived before I met you.

Then I rub two red plum petals together,
their dried blood dripping from my fingers
into a frozen stream.

I still see precisely how things stood
when your own heart burst into flames.

Wuhan

Listening to you lecture on T, C and the others

According to you
what really rattles
the fisher king
is a straight look
from his enemies' eyes:
if he locks onto them
he'll never again
kiss slippery lips
and jade breasts

In the dusty corridor later
you are just killing time:
do you mean what you say?
That's what I want to know
and what I intend to find out
night after night after night.
Which reminds me to ask:
where do you think you stand
on the question of mothers
and fathers? Fathers are vacant,
I think – mothers are women to them,
just women, that's all. Women.
What I always say is this:
mothers can even guide Buddha
through salt water to fresh.

Luojia Hill

Remembering things past

Once upon a time, when we were both
exhausted in bed, you whispered:
'I can even see you in the dark.'
I have loved those words for several lifetimes

already. It was the same day you brought me
a bunch of wild irises from Luojia Hill,
the day I told you, 'March rain is the best rain.'
I was born in March, not that you knew it then.

Now at long last I think you are missing me.

Double Shadow

You passed my door

Two stories up. On the one hand
not high enough to jump and die for you;
on the other, too low to rise above you and forget.

So I do neither.
Instead, I watch the moon yellowing into a cup
then drink it. This is the thousandth time today
I have slipped out of my world

into yours.
What else can I do, when you refuse
to follow me home? Will you never do that
again? Not once? Not when the locust flowers at last.

Harvest

A change of seasons

First
you counted how many Ming vases
there were in your house.

Next
you said: 'They're all thirsty.
They all need filling up.'

Soon
I was frightened of your blue eyes,
the blue that belongs in water.

Then
I wondered: 'Do you want me to check
each one every day? Really? Each one?

OK
I will.' And here I am now, rushing back
in time to see you punting across the river.

But
when I turn and glance from the steep valley-flank,
I notice the river is no longer running,

and
you are no longer you. A harvester is toiling
towards me, his scythe swishing the dry grass.

Dream

Your boat–shaped desk

In another minute I shall be smiling,
thanks to this noose in my hands.
In one minute. And after that, peace.

I have been thinking of the night
I heard your labouring whisper:
'O death, death, treat her kindly.'
Whoever forgets such things
is bound to lose their life.

With so much dark surrounding us,
how could I come back to you
now and not be noticed?

Zither Terrace

Seeing you've had L

Well, yes, the Englishwoman is pretty
and obviously grateful too.
Hence her winsome gush:
'He took me to the races!'
Now I'm alone at Zither Terrace,
Playing the keys in different time
and much too quietly for you to hear.
I tell myself: 'The beauty of Eastern music

is its monotony.' But I might as well talk
to the cold wind. I might as well let
the same wind hustle me downhill. Down
is the one direction I have left to travel.

Bridgehead

Waiting for your decision

The weight of that carved head
makes the whole bridge tremble:
what about the crowd gathering
there – can't they see the danger?
They can't. They're all looking forward
at something vague in the distance,
or staring at their feet picking a way
over the pine cones and concrete.

As for me, I must remember the head.
If I do, I might understand why the bridge
sways,
and brutally shakes me wide awake.

read more　🐧

HONG YING

THE CONCUBINE OF SHANGHAI

China, 1907. Sixteen-year-old orphan Cassia is sold by her aunt to a brothel. There, she works as a lowly maid for Madame Emerald until a powerful and dangerous client plucks her from obscurity.

Master Chang is the boss of the fearsome Shanghai Triad and he always gets what he wants. Despite her unbound feet and breasts, Cassia swiftly becomes Chang's favourite mistress. He showers her with luxuries as he embarks on her sexual awakening.

But Chang's world is violent and precarious, and those such as Cassia who depend on him are bound to his fate . . .

'A brilliant and sensitive writer' Jung Chang, author of *Wild Swans*

'A fascinating, full-blooded yarn which has the reader rooting for its heroine, a kind of Chinese Moll Flanders, every inch of the way' *Independent on Sunday*

'A beautiful and gripping writer' Tariq Ali, *Independent*

JENNIFER CODY EPSTEIN

THE PAINTER OF SHANGHAI

Based on a true story, *The Painter of Shanghai* tells the captivating tale of one woman's journey from a life of prostitution to the art studios of Shanghai.

At the age of fourteen Pan Yuliang, an orphan girl in the care of her opium-addicted uncle, finds herself in the third-class cabin of a steamship bound for a strange new town. When Pan and her uncle arrive in the city he sells his niece to 'The Hall of Eternal Splendour', where she is destined to live out her life as a prostitute in its smoky back rooms.

And yet, two years later, escape appears in the unlikely form of a government inspector who will take Pan as his concubine and introduce her to a glamorous new life in 1920s Shanghai: a life of love and of art.

But as Pan begins to realize her talent as a painter she also sees that she may lose something even more precious: a life of safety.

'A sparkling debut' *Vogue*

'Luminous...An irresistible story' *New York Times Book Review*

He just wanted a decent book to read ...

Not too much to ask, is it? It was in 1935 when Allen Lane, Managing Director of Bodley Head Publishers, stood on a platform at Exeter railway station looking for something good to read on his journey back to London. His choice was limited to popular magazines and poor-quality paperbacks – the same choice faced every day by the vast majority of readers, few of whom could afford hardbacks. Lane's disappointment and subsequent anger at the range of books generally available led him to found a company – and change the world.

'We believed in the existence in this country of a vast reading public for intelligent books at a low price, and staked everything on it'
Sir Allen Lane, 1902–1970, founder of Penguin Books

The quality paperback had arrived – and not just in bookshops. Lane was adamant that his Penguins should appear in chain stores and tobacconists, and should cost no more than a packet of cigarettes.

Reading habits (and cigarette prices) have changed since 1935, but Penguin still believes in publishing the best books for everybody to enjoy. We still believe that good design costs no more than bad design, and we still believe that quality books published passionately and responsibly make the world a better place.

So wherever you see the little bird – whether it's on a piece of prize-winning literary fiction or a celebrity autobiography, political tour de force or historical masterpiece, a serial-killer thriller, reference book, world classic or a piece of pure escapism – you can bet that it represents the very best that the genre has to offer.

Whatever you like to read – trust Penguin.

read more
www.penguin.co.uk